THE OTHER SIDE OF THE SUN

THE OTHER SIDE OF THE SUN

BARBARA NESBITT

Kids In Between, Inc.
409 Arbor Meadow
P.O. Box 1037
Ballwin, MO 63021

Cover: Gail Schenk

ISBN: 1-56734-082-2

DEDICATION

Dedicated to Maurice and youngsters like him who dream of escaping what life has unkindly handed them.   May all those youngsters find their way to happiness without giving up hope or without having to look on *The Other Side of the Sun* for the things they deserve and want from life.

CHAPTER ONE

Jean Bestie stood outside her classroom door. She smiled at Marilyn, the teacher who had become her closest friend at the school. They both waited for the long line of boys to file into the building. Marilyn was always assigned the smaller boys who were reading about fourth grade. Jean, who had a way about her that quieted even the tallest of the boys, was assigned the youngsters who were barely reading books for first graders. All were at least thirteen. Some were as old as seventeen.

Jean watched the boys enter the building. They wore what they all called their *scuz* uniforms. Blue jeans and light blue shirts. The thing they shared in common was delinquency and crime. No arsonists and no sexual offenders were ever assigned to the institution that sat at the end of a long road far away from the inner-city. Into the building marched the truants who had run the streets. There were boys who had long records of fighting, or knifings and shootings. They had records of stealing cars, burglarizing stores, or threatening their own families with weapons. Among the nearly one hundred youngsters, there were few offenses that one or the other of them had not committed at one time or another.

Despite the hardened lives most of them knew, they arrived at Morton Hills frightened. They had no idea what was ahead for them. Not a one among them hadn't heard rumors about horrible things that were done to the boys. It didn't take them long to overcome their fears and realize that every story they had heard had been invented by those who didn't know the truth or by those who enjoyed creating fear.

1

The men and women who supervised the boys in the cottages didn't beat them. The youngsters weren't made to stand naked while someone held fire hoses on them, and they weren't forced to go without food or sleep. Not one of the ugly stories any of the boys had ever heard while waiting to be transferred from juvenile detention to Morton Hills had turned out to be true.

Within a week after their arrival at Morton Hills their fears disappeared, only to be replaced by much of the anger and bad behavior that had led to their being sent to Morton Hills in the first place. They hated the rules that made them go to school everyday. They hated that they had no choice of food except what was put on their plates. They rebelled at having to be in bed by ten o'clock. For many, their coming to Morton Hills gave them their first taste of having to do what someone else wanted them to do. They had run free for too long. Their families and the schools had given up on them a long time ago. Learning that Morton Hills did not intend to give up on them was both painful and good. Until they learned that everyone at Morton Hills was not going to turn loose of hope for the boys, the youngsters fought against everything that Morton Hills was trying to do for them.

As Jean Bestie watched through the window, she could see a few of the boys talking and joking with their *Pops*. The men who ran the cottages, no matter what their age, were called *Pop*. Several of the wives of the men who headed the cottages didn't mind if the boys called them by their first names. It was mainly the older women who wanted to be called *the Mrs*. It usually took several weeks, or sometimes several months, before any of the boys cared enough about their Pops and the Mrs., to respect them and to do what was asked of them.

Putting their trust in others was not something the boys knew how to do very well. It was just so difficult for the boys finally to accept that the Pops and the Mrs. meant what they said and that they'd stand by their word. This held true if the cottage parents promised a given punishment for a bad behavior or a reward for good behavior.

Jean Bestie, like almost everyone at Morton Hills, had been given a nickname. Sylvester had been the one who, quite by accident, gave Jean Bestie the nickname of *Pesty Bestie*. Two years later it was Tommie Hicks who one day shortened Jean Bestie's nickname to PB. *Mrs. PB* was the name that he simply called out in class one day when he wanted some help, and within a matter of weeks, *Mrs. Bestie* and *Pesty Bestie* had disappeared from the mouths of her students and was replaced by Mrs. PB. In the years to come most of Jean's students came and went from her class never knowing her by anything other than Mrs. PB.

The nickname was not one that Jean thought showed disrespect. She almost thought of the name as one the students used because they liked her. In the fourteen years that she had been teaching at Morton Hills there had only been four boys who had to be transferred out of her class because she couldn't deal with them and they couldn't get along with her. The thing that her students came to accept about Jean was that she was fair. And despite all that had happened to the young boys who entered her classroom, she had learned that except for those who had serious mental illnesses, the boys also were fair. They'd argue with her and they'd threaten her, but in the end, when given time to think over what had happened and what she had done, they'd see that Jean was fair.

Their sense of fairness came back in ways that Jean also came to understand. She would have preferred more sincere apologies, but she knew that a youngster had gone as far as he could go when he'd stand before her with his head down and barely mumble that he was sorry. If a boy angrily stalked out of the room, yelling that he didn't have to do what she said or cursing how he was going to get her, Jean said nothing, preferring to wait it out. In fifteen minutes, in a half hour, in three hours, it made no difference, the boy would be back. If he came back, took his seat, and said nothing more, Jean accepted that he was offering her some form of an apology. Jean knew there was little point in forcing a formal apology or in embarrassing the boy in front of the other students.

All her students sensed where the line was that they could not cross. She could be as tough and as strong and determined as any who sat in her class. There was a willingness on her part to put up with a certain amount of their bad behavior while they adjusted to again being in school. Then it was as if she knew and they knew the day had come when bad behavior would have to end. One of her favorite phrases was, "Okay. It's over. Do you get my meaning?" She'd look right at the youngster. The tip of her finger would be on a shoulder as she spoke. The finger was like a symbol that she could touch them. The finger on the shoulder stood for the fact that they must now obey her and that they must stop misbehaving in school.

There were some boys who'd look back at her and warn her to get her finger off them. When their eyes met hers, they realized their words were wasted. They could see that she was going to win and they were going to have to behave. None of them would be able to offer a reason as to why they knew this, but it was commonly said among her students, "You gotta do what PB says." Or, "PB is someone you don't wanna mess with."

When a new student asked why, the answer simply was, "Because." If the new student still felt he had to prove himself, he'd scowl and say, "She better not be messin' with me."

The answer to that was, "You see who be messin' with who, man." The message was, they *had* to do what Mrs. PB said even if they didn't understand why. On the streets they had known people like Mrs. PB. A man in a hallway who told them to stop. And they stopped. Another youngster who told them to put something down, and they would put it down. The police officer who'd order them to move away from the corner, and they moved. That mysterious thing in the voice, in the way the words came out, and in the way these people looked were all signs that warned them they must do what they were told. That was the affect Jean had on them.

Unlike a few of the teachers at Morton Hills, Jean Bestie liked her job. The thing that she had understood from the day that she came to teach at Morton Hills was that she had such a

5

short time to work miracles. The teenage boys who ended up in Jean's class couldn't read. Many couldn't tell time. Half of them didn't know in what state they lived. So clever on the streets. So behind in school. The courts had sent them to Morton Hills for twelve months. Except for those youngsters who were almost beyond her help, and who had home situations that were so horrible they stood no chance of being released in a year, most of the boys were gone in one year. During that year many were not in school during the summer, they were out of class for sessions with social workers, there were trips to doctors, home visits, and suspensions for behavior in class that was not acceptable. In her countdown of time, Jean really had about seven months to try to raise their abilities so that perhaps when they left Morton Hills they could go to school and keep up with their class.

Along with the stories of her successes with the boys, there were the stories of the failures. Not her failures. What made her angry was not knowing who to blame for all the terrible things that happened to the children after they left Morton Hills.

Michael had been shot in the stomach while he stood on his front porch. Lionel had been stabbed because he fought with an angry attacker who wanted his ring. Johnnie's picture appeared on the front page of the newspaper. He had driven a car for a gang that robbed a bank and had taken a nun as a hostage. The wild police chase ended when Johnnie was killed when he crashed into a bridge that would have taken him across a river to another state. Jean remembered the day when Johnnie finally understood what states were and he had learned the names of all the states that surrounded Illinois.

The list of all the unkind and terrible things that had happened to all the boys who had passed through Jean's class was long. Sixteen were dead, mostly from gunshot wounds or knifings. Almost twenty-five of them had gone on to commit some serious crime that led to prison sentences. The whereabouts of those who weren't written about in the newspapers often remained unknown to her. Jean preferred to think that hopefully their lives had gone on and nothing bad had happened to them.

Now and then she'd meet one of the boys on the street or see a boy who had grown to manhood and she'd hardly know him. Like Vernon. Jean had been standing on the corner eating a hotdog. Suddenly she saw this tall, young man racing toward her. Jean placed a firm hold on her purse, believing that the young man was a mugger after her money. Breathlessly he called out, "Mrs. PB. It's me, Vernon. Remember me?"

Jean could not place him among the hundreds of young faces that had been in her class. She assumed that he *must* have been in her class. She didn't want him to think that he was so unimportant to her that she had forgotten him, and so she lied. "Of course, Vernon. I try to remember you all."

"You taught me to tell time. I still remember that dumb clock that had them funny hands on it. Remember I kept saying it was a baby clock."

"Yes." Jean smiled. The red and yellow plastic clock had belonged to her young nephew. The hands were shaped like legs and Vernon kept arguing that he couldn't learn to tell time

7

on a clock that had legs instead of hands. "It sure was a dumb clock." Now she could recall Vernon as a much smaller boy.

"I work at that place." Vernon pointed to a pizza parlor. "I used to clean the place. Mop the floors and stuff. Now I'm the cook." He smiled.

Jean felt pride for him. Vernon often talked about all the things he was going to buy when he had a job and became rich. Jean knew that Vernon really never seemed to understand how much things cost and how much money it would take to buy the things he wanted in his life. "It sounds like you're doing okay for yourself."

"I'm makin' it." Vernon shrugged. "I got me a wife now. She's gunna have a baby."

"Well, congratulations." Meeting a former student who was married and about to become a father was one of those reminders that made Jean aware how long she had been at Morton Hills.

"You still a teacher?"

"Yes, Vernon. I'm still out at Morton Hills and still fighting my battles."

"You're okay, PB. I kinda liked you after a while."

"Thanks, Vernon. I can always do with some good words."

"See, you."

He was gone as quickly as he had come. That's how it was with most of the former students whom she met quite by accident while shopping, at the show, or eating a hotdog on the corner on a hot, dry day. A few words were exchanged, and they passed out of her life as quickly as they had entered her life. Many of them thanked her or reminded her of some incident that had happened in class that she had long ago forgotten had ever happened.

Now and then she'd think how close she felt to them when they were in her class. It seemed as if she would never forget them and they would never forget her. Time wiped out so many memories for her and for them. When they were gone, they were gone. She'd sign the yellow paper they'd bring her, and she knew that next week their empty desks would be filled by other boys and she'd have to start all over. That was the way it was for her, and that was the way it was for the boys who marched into her classroom.

No matter how many came and went from her class over the years, Jean Bestie would always remember Maurice. There was a part of her that would always be sad because of Maurice. There also was a part of her that would also try harder with every boy who became her student because of what happened to Maurice. On the day that she heard the news about Maurice, she vowed that never again would she ever give up fighting for what was right for one of her students.

CHAPTER TWO

Three years had passed since Mr. Krueger, the principal at Morton Hills, had asked Jean to stop by his office during her lunch period. Mr. Krueger's general rule was to leave teachers alone if they were doing a good job. Visiting the principal's office was something that Jean seldom ever had to do. As she hurried down the hall, Jean reasoned that Mr. Krueger wanted to see her because he had a favor to ask of her. It was also one of Mr. Krueger's general rules never to demand or to order a teacher to do something. He believed that if teachers were asked, and if they believed they were doing him a favor, they were more likely to go along with what he felt was needed or wanted to make the school a better place.

Jean entered Mr. Krueger's outer office. Rose, the school secretary, was filling out a pink discipline form for Andrew. "Another little pinkie for you, huh, Andrew?" Jean smiled at the boy who used to be in her class, but who had been promoted to Mr. Nelson's class.

"I hate that..."

Jean cut him off, knowing that he was about to use curse words to describe his feelings toward Mr. Nelson. "You know what my answer to that one is, don't you?"

"Yeah." Andrew tried to smile but he couldn't. "Can it and cool it. That Nelson. He ain't even like a person. He's a..."

Again Jean raised her hand to silence him. "Mr. Nelson is probably in the teacher's lounge saying the same thing about you. It's all in one's perspective. Do you remember what I

10

told you perspective is?"

"That's all that there junk about how everyone sees things...like...uh...he don't got the same opinion or something."

"He *doesn't*, Andrew. You can't say *he don't*. And that's right. Everyone sees a situation from a different perspective or viewpoint. Mr. Nelson probably sees you as a mouth that won't quit running. From his perspective, you're a pain in the butt. Now what's your perspective, and leave out the swearing?"

"He don't..."

"*Doesn't. He doesn't.*"

"So. He doesn't know when to leave a guy alone."

"Ah," Jean smiled. "The question I have is, does the guy know when to shut up?" She pointed a finger at Andrew. "From my perspective, I recall you almost had to have a locked zipper on your mouth or you wouldn't be quiet. No teacher can teach if someone is steady running his mouth."

"He talks plenty hisself. He's always running his face."

Jean leaned over and put her face right next to Andrew's. "You know what, Andy? They pay him to talk."

"Somebody pay me to shut up and maybe I would."

Jean laughed. "I doubt it." She patted his shoulder. "Give it a try, Andrew. Go for one full day without talking in class and see if Mr. Nelson is on your case. You know what I taught you. You can't accuse people until you have proof."

"That that hypoth stuff?"

"Hypothesis. You start with a hypothesis, which is your belief. You come up with a theory or idea about your belief.

11

Then you test your idea or theory to see if it's right or wrong. Remember my theory was that you got out of your seat more than any other kid in the room."

"Yeah, and you was wrong. Darrell got up two times more than me."

"That's my point. I blew my theory. You gave me a chance to pick on someone else for awhile. So what's your complaint?"

"Mr. Nelson don't know nothin' about no hypothz."

"Hypothesis. And I bet he does." Jean turned to Rose who was smiling at the conversation that had taken place between Jean and the angry boy.

"My theory, Mrs. PB, is that Andrew and Mr. Nelson are *never, never* going to get along. I told Mr. Krueger he ought to move Andrew back to your class even if he has learned to read."

"Oh, no." Jean pretended to fall over. "Not that. Don't put that monster back in my class."

Andrew was grinning. "I ain't gunna go back in no baby class. You got a bunch of dumb babies in your class. Them empty-heads can't read or nothin' like me."

"I'll have you know, Andrew, the empty-heads and I get along very well, thank you all the same."

Rose added, "Wait until you see the empty-head Krueger has waiting for you." Rose nodded toward Mr. Krueger's office. "He's a winner, this one is. Whew. He's already been moved out of Pop Allan's cottage and into Mosley's."

"That bad?"

"Real bad."

Jean moved her eyes toward Andrew and then back to Rose, signaling that they shouldn't be talking about one of the boys in front of Andrew. Rose understood. "You can go right in. Mr. Krueger has been waiting for you."

Maurice was slumped in a chair across from Mr. Krueger. His long legs were stretched across the floor. He made no effort to move them as Jean stepped over his legs to sit in the chair that Mr. Krueger had pulled up for her. A deep scar ran down the right side of Maurice's face. The scar made white jagged marks along his cheek from just below his eye to his ear. His brows were thick and dark and pushed together in an angry look.

Mr. Krueger introduced Jean to Maurice. He said nothing. He only looked back at her. His look was as determined and as forceful as any look Jean knew how to give. "How do you do, Maurice?" Jean extended her hand as she believed she should show respect for her students by doing what was proper and by doing what one adult would do toward another.

Maurice let out a little puff of air and ignored her attempt to shake his hand.

"Mrs. Bestie, we have very little information on Maurice. Somewhere along the line his school records have been lost or misplaced. Central High has sent what they had. Maurice had been there about four months. There are a few test scores, but really, we're almost working from scratch. You seem to be able to get a pretty good handle on what these kids can do. I thought we'd try him out in your class."

She glanced up at Maurice. His eyes were filled with hatred. Jean knew that he could not possibly hate her for any-

13

thing that she had said or done because she had not yet said or done anything. It bothered her because she knew such a look was always on his face. Maurice appeared to hate everyone.

"I already have twenty-two in my class. I don't even know that I have a desk for Maurice." Trying to get herself excused from taking a boy into her class was not what Jean usually did. She glanced at Maurice again. A shiver ran through her. Jean did not want this boy in her class.

"Well, that isn't really a problem. I think we can find another desk." Mr. Krueger quickly understood that one of his favorite teachers was unwilling to take the boy. "Maurice, would you step outside? I'd like to work out some scheduling with Mrs. Bestie."

Maurice sat there for a minute or so. He looked back and forth from Jean to Mr. Krueger. Then in a toneless voice he said, "When I feel like it, I'll move."

Jean looked down at the floor. Here was another one who would fight to have everything on his terms. It was November. All those type of battles had come to an end in October. Her class was a good class now. The boys did their work. They didn't argue with her about everything. Except for a now-and-then scuffle over something that wasn't important, and that was quickly settled, her class was peaceful. Everything she knew about young boys told her that Maurice would bring all the peace and quiet to an end. He would be on an endless mission to disturb the class. He would not rest until he had frightened every boy in the class and until he believed his teacher would leave him alone no matter what he said or did.

14

Maurice finally stood up. He was nearly six feet tall. His body was strong. He put on his sunglasses, making sure that he glared at the two of them before he strutted out of the office.

"That walk. I can tell by the walk." Jean smacked at her leg. "He's got to prove himself, Mr. Krueger. He's got to be slow and cool. His terms. I can see it now. Nightmare alley! We haven't had one like him since that Davis boy. What was his name? Mitchell. Mitchell Davis. That one nearly put us all in a nuthouse, and I think this one comes from the same model."

"Strangely enough, Maurice's last name is Davis."

"I knew it. Someone has made a twin out of Mitchell and sent him here to haunt us. I hate to ask, but what's this one here for?"

"I hate to say." Mr. Krueger leaned back and poured himself the soda he had brought to his office for Maurice.

"It's that bad?"

"Pretty bad."

"Like what?"

"He cut his mother's arm for a start."

"Lord." Jean shook her head. "Was it his own mother or some woman in the house who called herself his mother?"

"No, this was his own mother."

"Great! We've got a kid who knifed his own mother. I can imagine what he's going to do to his teacher, which isn't going to be me. I can promise you that."

"And," Mr. Krueger went on, ignoring her protest. "He

was put out of Central for pushing his principal down some stairs and for throwing a chair through the plate glass window that was the principal's office before Maurice tore it up."

"Why didn't the courts try him as an adult? This isn't any little kid stuff. This boy is mean. If I saw him coming down the street, I'd cross over and go four blocks out of my way just so I wouldn't have to meet up with him."

"His mother wouldn't press any charges. She even changed her story and said her boyfriend had cut her. Then she said she fell on the knife. Of course, she's saying this with about eighteen stitches in plain sight. Besides, Maurice is only fifteen. It's not often they get tried as adults when they're fifteen. For a murder maybe. Otherwise we get them. You should know that."

"Fifteen! That kid is fifteen! What does his mother feed him. Giant pills. He looks like he's eighteen. And I'll lay you odds he acts like he's an eighteen-year-old. An eighteen-year-old who's been to prison for ten years and learned how it all goes down. Have mercy, please." Jean pleaded. "I've worked so hard with these kids who I have now. They're finally getting it together. I'd have less trouble than if you came in everyday and set my room on fire than I'm going to have trying to control him."

Mr. Krueger downed the last drop of his soda. "I know." He felt sympathy for her. "He has to go into someone's class. I can't see him with Mr. Nelson. Mrs. Wygant couldn't begin to handle him. She has enough trouble with the younger ones. He can't stay in shop all day."

"I don't wonder. He'd saw everyone into little tiny pieces.

16

Why me? What about Rita's class?"

Mr. Krueger tapped a pile of folders on his desk. "Within this little pile are the names of twelve new students. They're all on their way here before Thanksgiving. Most of them are going to have to be placed in Rita Morenza's class. These boys are all doing fairly well in school. They are just about on grade level. That's going to give her at least thirty-one in her class. It would be beyond reason, and certainly not fair to ask her to take another one. And another one like this one would be out of the question."

"You said, though," Jean kept trying to find some point, any point, that would keep Maurice out of her class, "that we don't have any test scores on him. For all we know, he could be reading at eighth or ninth grade."

Mr. Krueger laughed and gave Jean a knowing look. "What do you think the chances are of that being the case? Come on, Jean. Get real."

Jean tilted her head back and looked at the ceiling. "I know. In my heart I really know. Can't you just see me, Mr. Krueger? Maurice has barely squeezed his huge body into a seat, and there I am trying to teach him the alphabet. Ugh! A million, billion ughs."

Their conversation was interrupted by the sound of a chair thudding against the floor and Andrew yelling out, "What's wrong with you, man? You're crazy, man."

"It sounds like the beginning." Mr. Krueger said to Jean as he bolted for the door.

Maurice had taken the chair he was sitting on and slammed it against the floor until he broke the legs off. Rose instantly

17

put a call through to Pop Mosely's cottage. Mr. Krueger barely had his office door open when Pop Mosely walked into the building.

"Settle down, boy. And better attend to the settling right away." Pop Mosely stood well above Maurice. Maurice wasn't frightened even in the presence of a man whom Maurice had to understand could easily pin him to the floor in seconds.

"I been hit by some bigger than you." Maurice glared at Ron Mosely.

Ron took Maurice's arm and led him out of the office, "But probably not nearly as hard and I know, boy, not for nearly as long." Pop Mosley, who was not yet twenty-five locked his fingers tighter around Maurice's arm. "Now you and me are going back to the cottage and do some serious thinking." Ron Mosley would have preferred at times to use force and fear to make the boys behave, but he had learned that it made no sense to strike a boy while warning him not to hit others. Having been, as Ron described himself, a "hood of the streets," it had been difficult at first for Ron to hold his own temper in line when dealing with the screaming, cursing and swinging fists of those he tried to control.

"I ain't into thinking," Maurice answered in a low, but determined tone of voice.

"Then our minds got a way to go before they meet." Ron pushed open the door, dragging Maurice behind him.

Jean leaned against the wall. "I knew as soon as Rose said that Maurice had been put in Mosley's cottage that we had a walking, talking, cursing devil to deal with."

18

"Mosley's a tough nut to crack. He can handle it." Mr. Krueger walked back toward his office.

"It's not Mosley I'm worried about. It's me and my students."

"We can only try it, Jean. If he's just impossible, we might have to have Maurice put on permanent cottage clean up. Or, and I hate to do it, we might have to ask the courts to place him at Spencer Ridge."

"Ah. And if there's anything we need to make us feel like failures, it's filling out the forms that will send one of these kids to Spencer Ridge. What they don't already know about committing crimes, being mean, and getting out of step with the rest of us, they'll learn from their roommates at the pint-sized prison."

"We can't help them all, you know."

"I think Maurice is going to be one of them on the failure side of our lists." She dropped her head and sighed. In the end, she knew she'd have to take Maurice into her class.

At the end of the day Jean pulled her car out of the small lot behind the school. She drove to the end of the gravel path that led to the main driveway and stopped for a moment. She looked across the road at Cottage Five. Through the windows she could make out the shapes of boys moving about in the cottage that contained those young men who were the most difficult to handle. Someplace within that cottage was Maurice.

Jean gave a deep sigh as she moved her foot from the brake to the gas pedal and drove down the road toward the stone pillars that signaled the end of the property that was

19

Morton Hills. She knew the weekend would go too fast. On Monday morning she would have to return through the gate, walk down the hall to her class, and face Maurice.

On Saturday night she placed a call to Ron Mosley's cottage. Her hope was that Maurice had done what so many of the new arrivals did. "This is Jean, Ron. I have this hope in my heart, Ron. Answer my prayers by telling me that Maurice has run away."

"If he has, I'm staring at his twin. He's sitting here watching television."

"All puffed up like he owns the place, huh?"

"Exactly. I told him I might consider buying him a throne with my next paycheck so it would be easier for him to play king. He doesn't have much of a sense of humor."

"I figured as much. Thanks." Jean put down the phone.

Jean's husband Dale finished drying the dishes. "The place is getting to you again?"

"Not the place. It's a kid named Maurice."

"You always say that. Then the next thing I know you're telling me some story about how the kid is really okay. You'll be coming home with some Maurice stories before long."

"I think the story I'll be coming home with is that Maurice has killed me."

Dale put his arms around her. "It's not going to be all that bad."

Jean's face looked very serious. "I think it will be with this boy. He seems so filled with hate." Jean turned out the kitchen light and went right on thinking about the rage that seemed as much a part of Maurice's face as his nose and eyes.

20

CHAPTER THREE

As Jean knew he would, Maurice walked behind the other boys in her class. His steps were slow. He had not an intention in the world of hurrying or of being in class by the time the bell sounded. Jean fought a desire to warn him that the students had to be in their seats before the bell rang. There was no sense angering him before he even stepped into the room. The other boys looked at her to see what she was going to do when they heard the bell and saw that Maurice was still standing by the door. She had no choice but to say something. Jean could not let them see that he could get away with what they were unable to do.

"Maurice, you're new here" She wanted to make it clear to the others that she was going easy with Maurice because he had just arrived at Morton Hills. "The rule is, you have to be in the room and in your seat before the bell sounds." Jean knew that no matter what she said, if she spoke to him at all, it would be the beginning of a war that she didn't want to wage.

"Says who?" Maurice slouched against the wall.

Her years of teaching experience told her not to begin the battle now. Not in front of the other boys who would listen to every word and watch every movement to see who would end up holding the upper hand. "If you want to stand there, Maurice, be my guest. It's a long morning, though. I can assure you, the wall will stand up whether or not you lean on it. If you decide later on to sit down, that's your desk." Jean pointed to one in the back of the room near the window.

Casey started to speak out. He quieted himself and raised his hand, preferring not to get a demerit for calling out. When

Jean asked him what he wanted, she knew before he asked his question what the question would be. "How come he gets to stand there? You said we all gotta sit down."

Jean had no answer that would justify what she was allowing. "Casey, take it from me. The best thing you can be doing right now instead of worrying about me and Maurice is to bend your head over your paper that I'll be collecting in about twenty minutes. Is that registering with you?"

"I'm supposed to butt out, huh?"

"You got it."

Jean had made her way around to each student at least twice before Maurice flopped down on the floor and went to sleep. His long body stretched across two rows. The boys who passed over Maurice carefully raised their feet so as not to disturb him. They all sensed what Jean knew. Maurice was like a sleeping giant that dared anyone to wake him.

It was the lunch bell that stirred Maurice awake. He stood up and stretched just as Ron Mosley appeared at the door. "Did my new charge give you any trouble?"

Maurice glared at Jean. He waited for her to tell his cottage parent how he had spent the morning sleeping on the floor. The reply that he thought would come never was said.

"I don't expect much out of the boys the first week. Maurice didn't do any work, but that's to be expected." Jean waved her hand to signal to the other boys to file out of the room.

"If he gives you any trouble, give me a call. There's not a one of them from my cottage who needs to be causing any trouble at school."

22

"He'll do all right." Most of the time Jean welcomed the support and interest that came from the cottage parents. The cottage parents could ask as many questions as they wanted as long as they didn't make it seem that she couldn't handle her class. It would do her no good if her students believed it was the cottage parents rather than herself who controlled the class.

Ron walked down the hall with Maurice. Once Maurice turned around to look at Jean standing by the door. She didn't smile the way she would have with most of the boys. Her stare was as serious as that of the boy glaring back at her.

In the afternoon Maurice's behavior didn't change from what he had done in the morning. For forty-five minutes he leaned against the wall. Then he dropped to the floor and stared out the window as Jean worked with two boys on their reading.

Tyrone held the book close to his face, hoping if the book were closer, the words would come easier. He struggled with each word. "The man cl..The man cl..." He looked to Jean while he held his place on the word he didn't know.

"Clutched."

"The man clutched the bag. He ran done the street."

"Down. Down the street." Jean corrected Tyrone.

Tyrone went back to the beginning. "The man clutched the bag. He ran down the street. How did..."

"Who. It's not *how*. It's *who*."

Tyrone shook his head. "These words is hard. I liked that other book better."

"You've finished that book, Tyrone. You knew every word in it. Now it's time to move onto another book. Finish

23

the page, Tyrone. You're doing fine."

"He ain't doing fine, lady. He's a great big clown reading them baby books." Maurice flung his leg out and started tapping on Tyrone's leg.

"Hey, man. Whatcha think you're doing? Get them feet off me."

"I ain't bothering you, man. You just go on with your baby book." Maurice shoved his foot hard against Tyrone's.

"Don't be messin' with me, man." Tyrone backed his chair away from where Maurice was sprawled on the floor. "You ain't gunna be gettin' me in no trouble."

Jean stepped between where Tyrone sat and where Maurice had placed his leg. "Maurice, listen up. Now if you want to wear a hole in that floor sleeping, I don't care. If you want to stare out the window until the sun goes down, I don't care. What I do care about is this class. Every boy in here is trying his best. They've had enough problems in school already." She looked Maurice directly in the eye. "You do what you want to do as long as you don't bother any other person in this class. If and when the day comes that you want to start learning, I'll care about you and what you learn. For now, you stay out of my face and you stay out of the face of the other boys. Do you understand?"

"So send me to old man Krueger's office. I can handle that nobody."

"Mr. Krueger has more to do than step over your sleeping body. Take a nap, Maurice. Don't bother us." Jean turned her back on him.

The days that turned into weeks were not much different

24

than Maurice's first day. Everyday at lunch Ron Mosley asked how Maurice was doing. Everyday Jean told Pop Mosley that she was doing all right with Maurice. Maurice listened to the exchange of words between his teacher and his cottage parent, always expecting her to say that he did nothing in class and that he annoyed the other boys.

Though the boys argued among themselves, using threatening words to say what they would do if anyone touched them, or what was going to happen to the boy who moved a chair, or how someone was going to get someone else for staring at him, the words were empty threats that were never carried out. Jean allowed them to rid themselves of some of their anger by *mouthing* as she called it. They knew, though, there was a line they couldn't cross in Jean Bestie's class. None crossed it.

To prevent crossing the line that would get them in trouble, not one of them spoke to Maurice. No one in the class went near or touched Maurice's desk even though the boy had yet to sit in his desk. There wasn't a boy in the class who would borrow a pencil from Maurice or ask him a question about anything. They believed their only hope in avoiding a fight with him was to act as if he weren't there.

At the end of the fifth week of Maurice's arrival, Jean had grown weary of his body spread across the back of the room. She had made up her mind that sooner or later she would have to challenge him. The other boys never said a word to her, but they were sure that she was afraid of Maurice. They held their silence because they shared her fear. To go on letting Maurice do what he wanted to do, which was nothing, was unfair to

25

the other students. If the boys in her class thought no worse of her for backing away from Maurice, they thought no better of her for continuing to allow him to sleep most of the day in class.

The only clue Jean had which caused her to believe Maurice was not as sure of himself as he tried to pretend he was, lay in the fact that he had not once run away from Morton Hills. It was that point that she raised with Mr. Krueger. "Now you've been out here for...what is it? Twenty years?"

"Twenty-one years as of last April."

"How many kids have you seen come and go from here?"

"Hundreds upon hundreds. And I don't know if we were entirely wrong back in the old days when we got these kids up and had them milk cows and do some chores."

Jean didn't want to hear how it had been at Morton Hills twenty or so years ago. "Mr. Krueger, learning how to milk cows isn't much help when you live in an inner city."

He nodded in agreement. "But it taught them some discipline. They know everything now. You can't tell these kids of today a thing."

"I've got a point to make here, Mr. Krueger. I want to see what you think. Out of all those kids whom you've seen come and go, didn't most of them run when they first got here? It was almost as if they had to run away in order to prove a point. Then when they'd get caught and be put in their pajamas for a week, it's as if they took some pride in having run. Did you know that Maurice has not run?"

"So what's your point?"

"You're going to think this is crazy, but I think Maurice

26

likes it here. However bad he might think it is, there's something about this place that is better than what he came from."

"You surely don't think that he sleeps everyday, all day, in your class because he likes it here?"

"I don't know why he sleeps in class. Some youngsters sleep because they're depressed. Some sleep because the world is so terrible they'd just as soon be asleep and not know what's going on. I haven't figured Maurice out because he never says anything. I just have this gut feeling that there's some reason why he stays."

"And what are you going to do with your gut feeling?"

"I'm getting ready to make my move."

"Which means what?"

Jean picked up a stack of papers that needed grading. "Come Friday be on the lookout for an explosion. I'm going after him. I get the quivers thinking about what might happen, but I do know that I can't go on letting him lay there on the floor."

"Is he still bothering the other boys?"

Jean shook her head. "No. He cut that stuff out after about four days. I think he figured out he was on thin ice and it was just a matter of time before I said something to Pop Mosley. I wouldn't have, but Maurice didn't know that."

"Why don't you just tell Mosley that the kid isn't doing anything but mopping up the floor with his shirt and pants? Mosley will get him straightened out."

"And if it's Mosley who straightens him out in class, what do I do when Mosley isn't around? Come on, Mr. Krueger, you know better than that. If I can't control my class, it's all over for me." Jean put her hand on the doorknob. "Just be on your toes in case my plans to light a fire under the Floor Boy don't work."

On Friday morning Jean made sure that the other boys were busy with a writing assignment. She made a point of gathering them close to her desk near the front of the room. Jean glanced at the clock. It would be fifteen minutes before the lunch bell rang. Quietly she moved to the back of the room where Maurice lay on the floor tracing his pencil back and forth over a gray tile. She said nothing about the fact that he would have to wash off his scribblings. That could be handled on another day.

"Do you know that you've been in this class for five weeks?"

"So." He turned over on his back and thumped his foot against the bookcase. The books gently rocked back and forth as his foot touched the lower shelf.

"The fun and games are over, Maurice. I've let you act out your King of the Hill role long enough. You're not going to get it together on your own. By that I mean you're going to sit in that desk of yours and start seeing what you can do to help yourself or let me see what I can do to help you."

"I don't want nothin' from you, honky."

She ignored his remark about her being white. "But I want something out of you. That's the difference." She pointed her finger at him.

"Don't be stickin' no finger in my face." Maurice pulled himself up and leaned back on his elbows. He was aware now

28

that the other students were looking at them.

Jean turned around. "Do any of you have business with what's going on here?" She waited for any of them to dare to answer. "Then turn around and finish your papers." Her eyes didn't leave them until each one began writing again.

"Do you know what a theory is, Maurice?"

"No, and I don't care nothing about no theory."

"My theory, or idea, is you don't try to do anything in this classroom because you don't know how to do anything. You think you have to act tough. You make fun of the way the boys read. I'd lay you odds they all read better than you do. I'd also lay you odds that you can't read a word. Now what do you think of that?"

"Who you talkin' to? Not me. I can read."

"Then prove it, Mr. Mouth. Take any of those books. Any one you choose out of that bookcase. Read three words to me. Just three."

"I don't gotta do nothin' you say, honky. Not nothing."

Jean felt she was on the right track with him. Suddenly she realized she was right. She knew he couldn't read. "You won't do it because you can't do it."

Marshal called out, "What can't he do, Mrs. PB?"

Maurice moved quickly. He was on his feet and glaring at the boy. "Your mama."

"Don't be talkin' about my mamma. You surely ain't talkin' about my mamma." Marshal threw his pen down.

"Be cool, man." Julie warned his friend. "That dude's crazy." Julie held onto Marshal's arm. "Come on, man. He don't mean nothing."

29

"He doesn't." Lance corrected Julie as he often heard Jean do. "You're supposed to say *he doesn't*."

"You get your face out of my business." Julie turned on Lance.

"Stop it!" Jean stood up. She was angry with Maurice. It was his behavior that had led to the uproar. "Get your coats. The whole bunch of you. It's lunch time." Jean walked to the front of the room while the boys lined up. Then the bell sounded and they left the classroom. "Not you, Maurice. You and I are going to continue with our talk."

"I ain't missing my lunch."

"You'll stay as I asked." Jean moved over toward the door just as Ron Mosley appeared as he always did when the bell sounded.

"Get out here, Maurice."

"Pop," Jean faced the young cottage parent. "I'd like to talk to Maurice."

"What about his lunch?"

"Today he can miss it. We have some important things to talk about." The expression on her face told Ron Mosley not to push the fact that Maurice would not be leaving the school building for lunch in the cottage.

"You going to be okay with him?" Ron asked, knowing that there were times when he felt Maurice had something in him that could make him dangerous.

"I think it will be okay." Jean answered. She stood at the door until the halls were empty. Then she turned back to Maurice. "Okay, Mr. Mouth, it's you and me. You don't have anything to prove to anyone except me. Get out a book and read three...No. I take that back. Read *two* words."

"You ain't makin' me do nothin'." Maurice sat down on the floor.

"What is it with you and the floors?" She leaned over and took from the bookshelf what she knew was the easiest book in the entire classroom. She dropped the book in Maurice's lap. "Read two words."

Maurice picked up the book and threw it against the door. "Don't be puttin' no books on me, lady."

Jean reached down for another and dropped it in his lap. "Read even one word."

Before the book fell, Maurice grabbed it and threw it at Jean. "I told you, honky, don't be messin' with me."

Jean threw the book back at him. "One word. You can't read one word because you can't read."

"I can read anything I wanna read." Maurice stood up and kicked over a chair.

"You're angry because you know I'm right. Admit it, and I'll help you." Jean tried to look him in the eye but he wouldn't look at her.

"You're messin' with me. You're messin' with Maurice and that ain't good." He stood up and began pacing the room.

Jean followed behind him. "What's not good is that you can't read and you won't admit it."

Maurice flattened his hand and scraped all the papers off her desk onto the floor. "You're gettin' me riled, lady. Real riled."

"Are you angry because you can't read? You can't read one word. That's why you're angry."

Maurice turned around and grabbed her shoulders and started shaking her. He screamed. "You get outta my face. You hear. You get out of my face or I'm gunna bust you."

"You bust me and I'll go to the hospital and get flowers and candy and cards. You'll leave Morton Hills in handcuffs and end up being tried as an adult for assaulting a teacher. Now get your damn hands off me."

Maurice pushed Jean as he let her go. "You shut your face."

"Why? Because you can't read and you won't admit it. Not one word. Maurice, you can't read one word. You're going to be stupid and ignorant all your life because you can't read one word."

The tip of his finger spun the globe around again and again. Then he picked it up and smashed it against the wall. "That's what I'm gunna do to you, you don't leave me alone."

"Oh, no, Maurice. You're going to wipe off those marks that you keep scribbling all over the tile. You're going to pick up everything of mine you threw on the floor. You're going to straighten out the books you've pitched around the room. You're going to do dishes in the cafeteria until you've earned enough to pay for that globe. And that globe costs sixty-dollars. You're going to do all that. You're going to learn to pick up things and be a yes, sir and yes, ma'am, guy because you're too ignorant to do anything else because you can't read." Jean was no longer sure of what she was saying. She kicked at pieces of the broken globe. "You're ignorant because you can't read. You'll always be ignorant. Ignorant. Stupid and ignorant."

32

Maurice caught her wrist and yanked on her arm. "You honky. You're gunna get it. I'm gunna fix you." He twisted Jean's arm and forced her to kneel down.

With her free arm, Jean reached up and pinched the hair at Maurice's neckline between her fingers. Then she pulled as hard as she could. Maurice released her arm, but Jean kept pulling at the hair.

Maurice bent lower as if his slouched position would make the pain of her pulling on the hair stop. "Let go of me. Get your hands away from me."

"Admit you can't read!" Jean screamed at him.

He kept trying to pull away. She followed behind him, refusing to let go of his hair as he kicked over one desk after another. Then he stretched out his arm and yanked on her hair. "You like it? You like someone pullin' your hair?" Tears were falling from his eyes.

"No, but I can read. I can read and you can't read. Admit you can't read." She felt her hair being pulled from her scalp.

Their arms were wrapped around each other's heads as they now used two hands to pull one another to the floor. Maurice dropped to his knees. He held a thick wad of Jean's hair in his hands as he beat his fists against the floor. "I hate you. I hate you more than anybody."

Jean was crying. "I don't care if you hate me. I'll help you, Maurice. Admit you can't read, and I'll help you."

Maurice lay on his back and rolled from side to side. "Get out of my face. I hate you. I hate this place. I hate everyone."

"That's all right. Hate me. Hate Morton Hills. Hate the

whole damn world, but admit you can't read."

Maurice lay still and silent. Tears rolled down the side of his cheeks as he stared up at the ceiling tiles. Jean picked up the book that she had first dropped into his lap. "Read. Read any two words in the book."

He moved his head in circles as his wiped his nose and his eyes with the sleeve of his shirt. "I can't read."

Jean leaned against the wall and let out a deep sigh. "Thank God!" She noticed one of her shoes was missing. "I've lost my shoe." She rose up on her knees and looked around the room.

"It's over there." Maurice pointed. "By that there globe."

"You mean what *used* to be the globe."

"That thing don't cost no sixty-dollars."

Jean ran her hands through her hair. She felt the blood oozing down her neck from where Maurice had torn out the hair. "I think the school can get a discount. Maybe they're fifty-dollars."

Maurice noticed the blood running down onto her yellow sweater. "Here." He held out the hand that held the hair. "You want this back?"

"For crying out loud, Maurice. What am I going to do with a wad of hair that isn't in my head anymore?"

"You hurt my hair." He pouted as he tried to defend himself.

"You can't hurt hair, Maurice. I hurt the skin out of which your hair grew."

Jean heard the first bell sound. The students would be back in ten minutes. "Lunch is over."

"I didn't have no lunch."

"Well, Maurice, I wasn't exactly gorging myself on food this last half hour, either." She stood up. "If you think I'm going through this everyday, you're sadly mistaken."

"Did you mean what you said? I mean..." He bent down to pick up the broken globe. "You gunna help me?"

"I said I would and I will." Jean lowered her voice and put her hand on his arm. "It won't be easy. Learning to read is one of the hardest things you'll ever learn to do."

"So you ain't gunna help me?"

"Is that what I said?"

"No."

"Then why did you say that?"

"What?"

"That I wasn't going to help you?"

"I was askin'. Just askin'."

"I said if you would admit you couldn't read, I would help you. I always keep my promise."

"No one else ever did." The hard look that made Maurice appear so mean softened.

"You'll not leave my room until you can read. Not big books, of course. But you will be reading something. That I promise. Can you get my shoe before..?" The sentence went unfinished as the door swung open and Ron Mosley stepped into the room.

He looked at Jean. Her hair was messed up and hanging down her face. Blood was still running down her neck. She stood there with one shoe off as she pulled at the large hole in her hose. Maurice's shirt was torn and there was a patch of

35

blood on the back of his neck. Only two desks were standing upright. Papers and books were scattered all across the room. Jean and Maurice stood together as they faced Ron Mosley.

His eyes never stopped scanning the room as he demanded an answer to his question. "What the devil went on in here?"

Maurice handed Jean her shoe. She held onto Maurice's arm as she balanced herself while she slipped on her shoe. Jean looked around for the wastebasket. Then she pitched the hair. "We've been reading, Pop. What do you think we've been doing?"

CHAPTER FOUR

The early spring brought weather that was warm enough for Jean to take the boys outside for a walk down by the river. One of the things Jean loved most about working at Morton Hills was the river that flowed along the bottom of the forested area just north of the school. As soon as it was warm enough, Jean held about half her classes outside. During summer school, the boys seldom saw the inside of a classroom.

The outdoors was not something most of the boys appreciated when they first arrived at Morton Hills. They didn't like the insects and the creatures that now and then stumbled into view as the boys walked along toward the river. Young deer that stood frozen from fear at accidentally running across the same path the boys happened to take were less frightened than the youngsters who screamed in terror when they saw any of the four-footed animals.

Jean found it amazing that the youngsters who grabbed her and each other at the sight of a raccoon or muskrat were the same boys who fearlessly walked streets where gunshots were commonly heard and where others often lay in wait to take their money or other possessions.

Though her students constantly complained about the spring mud and wet leaves they had to trample through, when she asked if they wanted to go back, they all yelled that they did not. It was usually only a matter of weeks before her students discovered that running through the woods or wading in the river was fun. They screamed when their toes touched the still-cold river water.

"Can we cross, PB?" Sid called out.

"In a couple of weeks. It will be May before I can live with any of you falling in and floating to another state." Jean sat down on a log and watched them pitching stones into the water or trying to skim a rock along the surface.

Maurice didn't join the others. Instead he sat down and leaned his back against a tree. His face was tilted up toward the sun. Jean called out to him, "What are you thinking about, fellow?"

His face still looked like that of young boy who had been turned into an adult way before his time. "I was wonderin' where the sun goes."

"What do you mean, Maurice?"

"Like at night there ain't no sun."

"The sun is always there. It's the earth that is moving around the sun. It's called an orbit. The earth also rotates. Part of the earth faces the sun part of the day. When it's dark, it's because the earth isn't facing the sun. Do you understand?"

"I suppose." Maurice seldom would admit what it was he didn't know. He lived in constant fear that the other boys would find out how little he knew. He nodded toward some of the others who were climbing nearby trees. "Do them dudes know about the sun and the earth moving and all that stuff?"

"Some of them do. Some of them don't. I'm not sure that I understand all about it myself. I never was very good at science."

"I thought teachers knew everything."

"I got news for you, Maurice. We don't. I barely got through my science courses at college. To this day I don't know how I passed chemistry."

"What's chemistry?"

Jean thought for a moment. "It's about elements and compounds. Atoms. Everything is made of atoms. Did you know that? I mean you and the sun and me and this tree. We're all just a pile of billions and billions of atoms."

Maurice's seldom seen smile appeared. "You're makin' fun of me. I ain't that dumb."

"Oh, no." Jean assured him. "I'm not making fun of you."

"You tryin' to tell me that me and the sun is made out of the same stuff."

"It's true."

Maurice looked up at the sun. "The sun's all clean and shiny. I ain't like that." He folded his hands behind his head and closed his eyes. "You know what I wish?"

"What?"

"I wish I could get me on the other side of the sun."

Jean sensed such a feeling of sadness in his voice. "Why would you want to do that?"

"Cause I bet it's all clean and nice on the other side of the sun."

"You mean like no one has ever touched anything? I don't really know what you mean."

"I can't use the right words." Maurice thumped his foot on the ground. "I just think that if I had some kind of special ship like them astronauts use or something, I'd go in that ship and land in a nice clean spot where no one yelled and shot each other."

"Away from guns and police and druggies and dealers. Is that what you're talking about?"

"Yeah. I'd be the first one on the other side of the sun and I wouldn't let none of them land."

"What would you take with you?" Jean enjoyed talking with him and listening to what it was he wanted from life.

"Nothing. I wouldn't take nothing with me 'cept maybe my auntie."

"I've never heard you talk about your auntie. Is she nice?" Jean knew very little about Maurice. Years ago she stopped reading the records of her students. She didn't want to know what had happened in their lives before they came to Morton Hills. She didn't want to read about why they had been expelled from other schools or why the police had picked them up and why the courts saw fit to send them to the youth center. Some of who they were, and what they had done, came to her through Mr. Krueger, their cottage parents, or their social workers, but she made no special effort to find out too much about her boys. Jean was determined that she would judge the boys only on what they did in her class. Maurice and the few school records that followed him were treated no differently than she had treated the other boys and their records.

"I lived with my auntie before I came here. She was nice to me. Not like my mama. Ooh, ew! Now that's a bad lady, that mama of mine. My auntie, though, she cooks real good.

She tried to help me, but I..." Maurice looked back up at the sun. "I screw everything up. My auntie bought me clothes and everything. She tried to help me with my school, but I liked that glue too much. My auntie told me to cut it out or get out."

"You were a sniffer?"

"Um." Maurice stretched out again. "That felt so good. That glue hit my nose and my problems," Maurice waved his hands in front of him, " and my problems just disappeared. Gone. Zap. Zap. All gone."

Jean called out to Danny to get away from the edge of the river. "I can see that." She smiled at Maurice. "That's why you're here. You got rid of all your problems and you just showed up here for a little vacation."

"Is it true, Mrs. PB, that some folks go on vacations? Like they go to other places and lay out in the sun and go on those there big boats. I seen that stuff on TV, but I figure them commercials is lying."

Jean laughed. "I get that same feeling myself. Yes, Maurice. People do go to other parts of the country or even to other parts of the world."

"But nobody ever goes to the other side of the sun."

"I promise if I hear about anyone making that trip, I'll let you know. In fact, I'll ask them to take you along."

"I don't want nobody goin' along. Just me and maybe my auntie."

"I think that's enough blowing in the wind for today. I have to get the troops rounded up. We have some studying to do." Jean walked closer to where the boys were chasing each

41

other and throwing rocks. "Listen up. Roll those bodies over here. We're walking up that way. " Jean pointed to the lowest of the hills at Morton Hills. "And we're going to be talking about river currents and tributaries today."

Adam stepped up his pace so that he could walk with Jean. "Ain't nobody wants to learn about no tribu...whatever them things is. We wanna play."

"Don't we all, Adam. I'm not paid to play. I'm paid to teach."

"We ain't gunna tell no one."

Jean rumpled Adam's hair. "I don't trust you little liars and thieves. You'll turn me in and I'll lose my job. The next thing I know you'll have a smart teacher. Maybe a pretty one. I can't risk it."

"Did you used to be pretty? When you was young?"

His honesty made her laugh. "I'm only thirty-eight, Adam. I'm still walking up these hills. Or do you think I should be in a wheelchair?"

"Thirty-eight!" Adam turned around. "Hey, man. PB is thirty-eight!"

She listened to them talk about how old she was as they made their way to the hill. "If you guys think I'm old, wait until you find out how old this river is. We're talking millions and millions of years old."

"There ain't nothing that old." Nathan challenged her.

"Oh, yes, there is." Jean sat them down on the hill and they talked about how rivers formed. The thing they liked most was listening to how the land was once covered with ice and how the mastodons roamed the land where they now sat.

The children were not like others believed them to be: Disinterested in life and the world. They came to care about many things, but they couldn't care until they finally believed that someone cared about them.

Maurice had been among the hardest to convince that someone cared. Every time he came to words in the books that he had to struggle through, he became angry. He was sure that Jean wouldn't care about him if he didn't get the words right. Rather than wait for her to yell at him, he yelled first. He cursed the books. Sometimes he threw the books. Jean would wait for him to calm down. Then he'd get up and get the book and bring it back to his desk. It took him nearly a month before he would say the words above a whisper because, just as he waited for Jean to say something bad about his efforts, Maurice also waited for other students to laugh at him. Maurice finally accepted the fact that Jean wasn't going to say anything bad about his reading, and that she wouldn't allow other students to make fun of any other student. Until Maurice understood her purpose, he sat off in a corner by himself.

Each night Maurice took a list of five words to his cottage. Jean had told him the words he was learning were called *sight words*. "There are two hundred and twenty of them, and it's important that you learn them all."

"I know some of them. Here." Maurice pointed to a few of the words on the list. "I know this word is *the*. This is *on,* and *off*. There's a whole bunch I know."

"All of them Maurice. You need to learn them all."

Georgette Mosley would sit with Maurice after supper and

43

help him memorize the words. His cottage mother had far more patience than Pop Mosley. Georgette stepped in when she saw that her husband Ron was too quick to lose his temper when Maurice would forget the words. "It doesn't do any good to tell Maurice that you just told him the words. Believe me, Ron, if he knew the words he'd say them."

"How can he not know those words? My nephew knows them and he's only six."

"Maurice would love to hear that." Georgette scolded. "PB says that Maurice can't even read first and second grade books. That's why she sends these words back to the cottage with him, or are you missing the point?"

"I'll tell you what the point is," Ron paced the floor. "Someone ought to hold a gun to their heads and make them stay in school. All they know how to do is run the streets and stir it up."

"Look who's talking." Georgette grinned. "As I recall you spent more time on the streets than you did in school."

"And what did it get me? I still had to go back and graduate. Twenty-one years old and I was still in school."

"Because no one could tell you a thing when you were sixteen. Maurice isn't any different."

"Well, I'll tell you one thing, Georgette, I could sure read better than these kids even if I didn't go to school. I don't think Maurice pays attention half the time. He'd make a good space cadet."

"It's hard to pay attention when you don't understand what's being said. From now on I'll help Maurice. You can

44

spend the time you save helping him by walking around telling everyone what's wrong with the world." Georgette enjoyed teasing Ron.

Ron put his arm around his wife. He brushed aside her hair and gave her a kiss on the cheek. "I'm lucky to have you. You're good for me."

Georgette laughed. "I settled the wild and crazy man down, huh?"

"I needed settling."

Maurice stood in the doorway watching his cottage parents. Except for the kindness of his aunt, Maurice didn't know what it was like to see a man and woman be gentle and loving to each other. Ever since he had come to Morton Hills and saw how couples could care about each other, Maurice had decided that he would like to find a girl like Georgette. "Is you ready, Mrs?"

"Maurice," Georgette took the boy's hand. "You've got to clean up your language. You're supposed to say, 'Are you ready.'? Can you remember that?"

"You sound like PB. Not two words comes out of my mouth and that lady is ready to tell me what's wrong with them two words." Georgette's hand felt warm and soft. Maurice had come to like it when Ron put his arm around him or when Georgette smiled and touched his hand.

Both of his cottage parents felt as if they were getting to know Maurice better. Each believed at last they were getting through to Maurice. Several months later when Maurice went on his first weekend pass and brought drugs back with him,

Ron raged, cursed and stormed around the cottage. Ron felt as if he been betrayed. Georgette showed her disappointment and hurt by crying.

Maurice had secretly tried to sell the drugs to the other boys in the cottage. As with any act that went against the rules, there was always some boy who would tell what he had seen or heard. Before Ron could take Maurice to the administration building to face the punishment he would have coming, Maurice broke the lock off the cabinet that held the boys' canteen money, took what didn't belong to him, and fled from Morton Hills.

Jean would not accept what Maurice had done. She argued with Ron and Georgette in defense of Maurice. "There's more to the story. I'm telling you there's something going on that we don't know about."

"I don't think so." Ron assured her. "That kid made too quick of a turn around. It was like it was too good to be true. He probably was mixed up in drugs before he came here. Why is it so hard for you to accept the fact that he probably went home to his aunt's, met up with some of his street pals, and brought drugs back here to sell? Every kid in the cottage says he did it. Now who am I supposed to believe? They all can't be lying."

Jean frowned. "I just don't want to believe that he did it."

"Come on, Jean." Ron waved his hand at her. "The snitch said he did. Then the other boys backed him up. Since he wasn't going to get any money for the drugs because I had the drugs, Maurice had to get the money out of the canteen. Those hoods out there want their money. My books showed he had about ten dollars in his own canteen account from working in the kitchen. He got about two hundred out of the canteen. He's going to come up short when Mr. Pusher sticks out his dirty hand and wants his bucks. Maurice is going to have to hit the bricks again to peddle his products so that he can pay off what he owes. I'm telling you, Jean, Maurice is going in deeper before he gets caught."

"What's hard to understand," Jean argued, "is why it all happened in the first place. Maurice was doing well in school. I think he was adjusting to Morton Hills. In fact, I still say he almost likes it out here. Something must have happened when he went home. I just know that he didn't just decide on his own to get involved in drugs."

Ron kept shaking his head. "Don't make excuses for him. He had some choices. He made a bad one, and he'll pay for it."

Georgette felt sorry for Jean. As fair as Jean tried to be with all the boys, Georgette knew that somehow Maurice had become special to her. "You know he's going to get picked up again. He'll be back. We'll find out what happened."

Jean asked, "This aunt he talks about. Do you know anything about her? I mean is she okay or what?"

"I think she's his great aunt or something like that. She's in her fifties at least." Ron answered. "I've never even seen her except for the picture Maurice has in his wallet. I just figured she was too old to be his mother's sister. His mom is only about thirty-five or so. Why do you want to know?"

"I'd like to have a talk with Maurice's aunt. Maybe she knows where's he at. Maybe she knows how all this drug business got started again. And, you know what?" Jean recalled her conversations with Maurice. "He never used that stuff himself. He talked about sniffing, but I never did hear him say a word about crack or uppers or all that other garbage they pop and push into themselves."

"One usually leads to the other," Ron added. "They all got to start with something. Then they move right on up to the hard stuff. Maurice probably isn't any different. Kids sniff. Maurice isn't a kid anymore. It's just a matter of time before the white powder catches on with him. It always does."

"For crying out loud, Ron, he's only fifteen. He's a kid." Jean didn't like it that Ron seemed to have no understanding of Maurice's problems.

"Not on those streets he isn't. He's a man out there."

"Then we'll get him off the streets so that he can be a kid."

Georgette warned, "Don't get your hopes up Jean. And besides, he's going to face some heavy discipline when he gets back. Selling drugs in the cottage isn't exactly something that goes over too big with the superintendent out here."

"You're right about that." Ron headed for the door of Jean's classroom. "Maurice is going to need about six shovels to dig himself out of this one."

CHAPTER FIVE

Loreen really didn't want to let Maurice in. Not only did Loreen not like his face, she thought he was dirty looking. "Carminetta ain't home yet." Loreen stood in the door to block his entering.

Maurice made an attempt to smile at Carminetta's sister, but her look told him that his smile was not welcome. "I brought some stuff by for the baby." Maurice lifted his arms that held the many packages. "See. I got all this for her baby."

As much as the baby needed things, Loreen was sure that this was just another boy that Carminetta was using. "You can come in, but I don't want you hanging around here. Put the stuff over there." Loreen pointed toward a playpen. "Just set it in there." She watched Maurice, who looked very ill-at-ease.

"When's Carminetta comin' back?"

"Who knows? She runs them streets day and night. She thinks I got nothing better to do than watch her baby. I got homework to do." Loreen turned to walk out of the room when she heard the baby cry. She brought him back to the living room where Maurice still stood by the playpen. "Marvin's got the stomach cramps. Carminetta was supposed to get his medicine. She ain't come back all day." Loreen rubbed the crying baby's stomach.

"You tell me what to get, and I'll be on my way to get it." Maurice poked his head around so that he could see the baby better. "He sure is a little dude."

"He'll be six months in July." Loreen smiled back at the

baby who reached a tiny fist toward her face. "Carminetta don't deserve him. Marvin's a good baby and Carminetta don't look after him or nothing." She set the baby on the floor and changed his diapers. "You mean it about getting his medicine?"

"Sure."

Loreen ordered Maurice to turn around and face the wall while she went for her money. "I don't want you knowing nothing about where I keep my money."

"I ain't interested in none of your money. I got my own money." He dug into his jacket pocket and pulled out a handful of bills. "I got plenty of money."

"Junkie money." Loreen sneered at him. "I seen plenty of that kind of money, and I don't want no part of it."

Maurice looked at Loreen. She wasn't nearly as pretty as her older sister, and not a bit gentle the way Carminetta was. "You go to school?"

"Yeah. I like school."

"I hate school."

"That figures. Having a pocketful of junkie money and not liking school sort of goes together. Now me, I want a man who's gunna be something someday."

"Them dealers, they got plenty. They're somebody."

Loreen turned on him angrily. "They ain't nothing. They're hanging around on Wednesday acting all big and smart. Then on Thursday they is in jail, and on Friday most of them be dead. That ain't my idea of no man."

Maurice grinned, "But they sure had a pile of dough on them other days."

"Wipe that grin off your dumb face. You ain't funny. Them dealers is no good, and that includes you. Now go get the medicine for Marvin like you promised."

He took the money. "I ain't no dealer. I did a little hustling to get some money like Carminetta asked me. She said the baby was doin' without so I..."

"Hey, boy." Loreen yelled. "You mean them boxes is filled with things for Marvin that you bought with junkie money?"

"What's the difference? Marvin don't know no difference."

"I do." Loreen opened up the door. "Now you get out and take that stuff with you. Ain't none of us so poor we got to take drug money."

As Maurice bent over to take the packages from the playpen, Carminetta walked through the door. "Why, Maurice, honey. I didn't even know you was coming by today. Ain't he a sweet one?" Carminetta looked at Loreen and winked.

"I don't care if you are my sister, Carminetta. You're trash. Just street trash."

"Shut up." Carminetta screamed at her. "You surely not be talkin' to me like that. I mean surely not, girl."

Loreen picked up the baby and walked toward the door. "I don't suppose by any chance you remembered Marvin's medicine."

Carminetta put her hand on Maurice's arm. "That girl! She's enough to run me nuts. Harping all the time about that there baby. Like he's somethin' important."

51

"He's your son." Loreen wrapped a blanket around the baby. "I'm taking him outside. He don't need to be around *two* pieces of trash."

Maurice watched Carminetta as she stood in front of the mirror running a pick through her hair. She seemed so different around her sister than she was when they were alone. There weren't many girls that Maurice had ever seen who were prettier than Carminetta.

"See what I have to put up with." Carminetta flopped down on the couch. "That brat thinks she's so much better than the rest of us. Mama's always saying how Loreen does this. Loreen does that. Always talkin' about how Loreen does so good in school. I surely don't want to hear all that. What about me is what I want to know. One of these days me and my baby is gettin' out of here. And you, darlin', might be just the one that can help."

Maurice loved it when she called him *darling*. "I'd do about anythin' you asked me. You know that." He sat beside her on the couch and threw his arm around her shoulder. "Just tell me what you want and I'll be doin' it." Maurice couldn't believe that in only two weeks he had fallen in love and felt that whatever he had done in the past had no meaning and whatever he'd do in the future was unimportant compared to being with Carminetta.

She dangled her high-heeled shoe from her toe. "Is that stuff for the baby?" She smiled a big smile. "Why you're the sweetest thing. You done bought all that for my baby." Carminetta gave Maurice a quick kiss and then ran toward the packages, tearing them open without even bothering to look. "Ain't Marvin goin' be somethin' in these outfits? He'll really be somethin'. All blue. He just loves blue."

Maurice wished that she had taken more time to open each package instead of ripping them open and pitching the clothes on the floor. "Does Marvin know his colors?"

"Huh? What you talkin' about?"

"You said he loves blue."

"Aw. Forget it, darlin'. I was just jokin'. You're just too heavy sometimes, Maurice. Just too heavy for me. You need to lighten up and flow a little more easier." She came back to sit beside him. "I sure am a lucky girl to have you." She ran her finger along the side of his face. "Poor, Maurice. My poor little baby with all them there bad cuts. I just want to cry thinkin' how somebody hurt you."

"My mama's boyfriend did that. I hated him about more than I ever did hate anyone."

"Where's your mama at?"

"Over on Kennet Place. I'm hidin' out in her basement."

"Surely not. What you hidin' from? The police after you or somethin'?" Carminetta didn't want any trouble to come to her because of this boy. "You ain't in any kind of trouble, are you?"

If she found out that he had run from Morton Hills, she'd know that he wasn't eighteen as he had told her he was. Maurice was sure that a girl of seventeen wouldn't want a fifteen-year-old for a boyfriend. "Some dude says I owe him. That ain't true. He owes me. I gotta lay out for a while until it blows over. No big deal."

"Now don't be bringin' no trouble to my doorstep. My grandma she let me and mama and Loreen stay here because it's close to the brat's school. My grandma ever find out I hangin' out with some troublemaker and she be puttin' us out."

Maurice frowned. "Yeah. I be hearin' you." He hated it when Carminetta was anything but sweet.

Carminetta looked at his scowling face. "Hey, boy. You're my man. Don't be frettin'." She linked her arm through his. "You gunna have time to party tonight? I got me a new dress. Whew! Wait until you see my dress! It's somethin'. I mean really somethin'."

"Where we partyin'?"

"I know these dudes on the other side of Toliver. Coolest you'd ever want to meet."

The last thing Maurice wanted was to spend an evening with other men whom Carminetta knew. "I thought we was gunna be by ourselves. I don't wanna do no partyin' with no dudes."

"Sure, honey. We'll do somethin'. Just you and me." She didn't want to make him angry. He was going to be too easy to use. Getting him upset was not something she wanted to do. "You know how you said you'd do about anythin' for me. Did you mean it or is you just running your face to make me think you're a big man?"

"I mean it, Carminetta. You ain't like no girl I ever seen."

"How about I give you a list of a few things for me? You done good by me and Marvin. Now how about you look after your girlfriend." She snuggled close to him. "You want your lady lookin' good, don't you?"

"That's how I want it." In many ways Carminetta frightened him. She seemed so grown up. Maurice was afraid to say much to her for fear she'd discover how little he knew. "You make me out that list. I'll see that you be gettin' everythin' on it."

Carminetta squealed with laughter. "Everythin'?"

"Everythin'."

Maurice looked over the list that she had written out. He could read a few of the colors and he knew the words *dress* and *jeans*. Most of the words on the list were unknown to him. He folded the paper up and put it in his shirt pocket. "It's as good as done." He hugged Carminetta and gave her a kiss. "You're really my lady?"

"Always and forever." Carminetta walked him to the door. "You ain't never had no better lady than Carminetta." She watched Maurice run down the stairs and out the front door of the building. Then she closed the door. Carminetta leaned against the door and smiled. She was very happy with herself that she had found this young boy whom she thought of more as a dumb pet than a boyfriend. For several minutes she stood in front of the mirror and imagined how she would look in all the things that he would bring her.

Loreen sat huddled at the foot of the stairs. She was rocking Marvin in her arms when Maurice passed. "You won't be lookin' so happy by the time Carminetta gets done with you."

"Hey, girl. Why don't you quit bad-mouthing your sister?"

"She's using you and you're too stupid to see that."

"She ain't usin' nothin'. Carminetta loves me just like Georgette loves Ron. Now I got me my own lady."

"You ain't got nothing except a list I bet."

"Whatcha talkin' about?"

"Carminetta makes out lists for her guys. When she gets a few of her lists filled, she dumps the guy. She'll dump you. You wait and see. Carminetta doesn't just like men. She likes *all* the men. And you, dude, stand even less of a chance because you're a boy."

"I ain't no boy."

"You ain't no man, either." Loreen sneered at him. "You're just a street creep and you ain't gunna amount to nothing."

"Says who?"

"Me."

"And who you think you are?"

Loreen shrugged her shoulders. "Nobody important right now, but I'm gunna be somebody someday."

"What makes you think so?"

"Because I don't wanna live here no more. I don't wanna be poor. And I don't want junkies hanging around where I live. I want a man who ain't gunna run out on me first time he sees another lady he likes, or he's got some deal going down out on the streets so he's gotta run and take care of his deal, or he's gotta run and hide 'cause something went wrong with his deal. Ain't no way I'm gunna live like that."

56

Maurice felt the color rush to his face as she described someone much like himself. "What makes you think you're somethin' special that you gets all that you want?"

"I ain't never gunna get all I want, but I sure gunna have more than I got now." Loreen lifted Marvin up so that his head rested on her shoulder. She patted his back and rocked the body back and forth to soothe his whimpering. "I ain't gunna have babies until I'm full grown. I'm gunna go to school and get me an education like my grandma says. Someday I'm gunna have a good job. And I'll tell you somethin' else, street creep, I don't want no man like you."

"Ain't nothin' wrong with me."

"That's an opinion. My opinion is you ain't no better than the rest of them I see hanging around here." Loreen looked up at the couple fighting in the hallway. "See. You think I wanna live around that noise and that fighting. I wanna go where it's clean and nice."

Maurice smiled at her. "Like on the other side of the sun?"

"Whatcha talking about, boy? Other side of the sun. No one lives on the other side of the sun."

"Maybe someday. You just might be surprised. Maybe someday. See you around."

"Not if I can help it." Loreen stood up to go upstairs. She looked at Maurice one last time. She felt sorry for him because he wasn't like the others that Carminetta used. There was something about Maurice that seemed decent.

57

CHAPTER SIX

Jean pulled her car up to the curb in front of the building where Maurice's aunt lived. The house was in a neighborhood that was on the edge of a very dangerous, run down neighborhood. The lawn was mowed and there was fresh paint on the front of the house. Somehow Jean had expected that Maurice's home would not be nearly as nice as the one that she sat staring at. There was a woman sweeping the porch. Jean walked to the edge of the steps and introduced herself. "I'm Jean Bestie. I'm a teacher at Morton Hills. I was wondering if you might be Maurice's auntie."

"I could be." She went on sweeping. "But then I might not be. What is it you're wanting?"

"He's run away from Morton Hills."

"He's not here." Flo Harris didn't trust the white woman.

"I'd like to help him, Mrs.... Maybe it's Miss." Jean extended her hand. "He was doing so well in school. I think he's in some kind of trouble."

Flo leaned on the broom. "I'm not sure if I know of a time when he wasn't in trouble. It's not his fault. The boy never stood a chance what with that crazy mother of his." Flo looked past Jean, staring sadly down the street at nothing in particular. "Sometimes, though, I think the woman probably did the best she knew how given her background. Pitiful. She's not right in the head. If you know what I mean. Drugs. I think she's probably burned up most of her brain." Flo stopped speaking. She felt she had already shared more than she wanted to tell the woman who said she was Maurice's teacher.

58

"I'm sorry." Jean didn't know what else to say. "I thought maybe you might have some idea where Maurice is. His cottage parents told me that he came here on his furlough. When he came back he brought drugs with him. He sold them to the other boys in the cottage. Then he ran. I'd like to find him. I really think I can help. The staff at the school can help him. We all want to do something to save that boy."

Flo watched Jean as she spoke. There was something about the pained look on her face that made Flo believe the woman meant what she said. Flo welcomed any help she could get. She was weary of trying to straighten out Maurice all by herself. "Would you want to come in? I can fix us some coffee or tea."

Jean was relieved. She knew the woman hadn't trusted her. "That would be nice."

"I'm Florence. About everyone I know calls me Flo. Florence Harris. And I'm not Maurice's real auntie." She opened up the screen door and led Jean into a spotlessly clean living room.

The first thing Jean noticed was a picture of Maurice on the mantle over the fireplace. "How old was Maurice in this picture? He looks like he's about ten or so."

"That he was." Flo picked up the picture and held it in her hands. "I had a great deal of hope back then. My hopes have grown a lot thinner lately." She motioned for Jean to sit down. "I'll fix that pot of coffee. Or would you rather have tea?"

"Whichever is easier." Jean sat down on the sofa. She could hear the clatter of cups and then the whistling teapot.

Flo set down a tray filled with cookies and fruit. Then she poured the tea. "Cream?"

"No. Just plain." Jean took the teacup that Flo handed her. "You said you weren't Maurice's auntie. Are you related to him at all?" The woman was so refined that Jean didn't understand how she could be part of Maurice's family.

"No kin. I used to live in the same building where the mother stayed. She's always been a junkie. The whole time she carried Maurice she went right on using drugs. One night she came pounding on my door. She was screaming that the baby was going to be born. I opened that door and there she was. All glassy eyed and shaking." Flo sipped her tea. Her eyes brimmed with tears. "Here she was about to give birth to a baby and she's still putting all that junk in her. It was enough to make a person sick just looking at her. You want more tea?"

"Just a half a cup." Jean held the cup out.

"Maurice was born about six weeks earlier than he was due. Born an addict. Pitiful. Purely pitiful. His mother didn't take care of him like she should have. Young and crazy and wild. It turned out I had Maurice half the time. No. *Most* of the time. That little fellow grew up thinking I was his mama. He finally figured out that I wasn't his mother. Then he took to calling me Auntie Flo. My own young ones were grown and gone. I didn't mind having that little boy around at all.

"Then the neighborhood kept getting worse and worse. It was a sad day when I moved away from Maurice. I had to. I simply had to get away from all that nastiness. All those drugs. Pitiful." Flo shook her head in disbelief.

"But you still saw Maurice, didn't you? He still talks about you."

"Well, bless his heart." Flo smiled with pride. "Oh, yes. He'd come and stay with me now and then. That mother of his took up with some bad ones. Poor little Maurice would get locked out of the house or he'd be without food. It's that mother who should have been locked up. Not Maurice."

"And school. How did he do in school?"

Flo turned a frowning face toward Jean. "Now how would you expect that little boy would do in school? Terrible. That's what he did. Just terrible. I'd try and help him with his letters and his numbers. He was slow to learn. All those drugs his mother took when she was carrying him, and what with being born an addict, Maurice had some serious problems. It was like she damaged his brain with her drug addiction. Just so sad." Flo bit her lip to keep from crying. "It wasn't fair to that child. Not one bit fair.

"From the day he started school Maurice had difficulty. He tried, bless his little heart. After a while he quit trying. Then he got in one mess after another. I even went to school for him a few times. I'd try telling him that he just couldn't act up so badly in school. Some of his teachers were kind to him. They tried as best they could, but Maurice was getting harder and harder to handle. No home training. His mother just let him run the streets.

"When he was about ten," she pointed to the picture, "or about the time that picture was taken, his mother got herself straightened out for a couple of months. She was going to get herself clean. She signed herself into one of those rehab places. It didn't last. She wasn't an hour back out on those streets and she was shooting up and snorting."

Jean smiled at Flo. It seemed strange for such a dignified woman to use those words. "Didn't she ever try to help Maurice?"

Flo leaned forward. "I'll tell you how crazy that lady was. One of Maurice's teachers told her that she needed to spend some time reading with him. Like get some books and help Maurice learn how to read. Well, now, wait and hear what that one did. She has one of her men friends buy a set of encyclopedias. A whole set mind you. That must have cost that man about three hundred dollars or more. Then she gets hold of Maurice and tells him to read the books to her that she bought him." Flo put her hand to her head and leaned back into the couch. "Plain craziness. Maurice barely knew his letters and here she's screaming at him to read to her."

Jean bent her head down. She felt sick to her stomach thinking about what Maurice had already been through. "Didn't she realize that he couldn't read?"

"She was so high all the time she couldn't figure out anything. That crazy woman had her man friend tie Maurice up in a chair. She put an encyclopedia in his lap and kept screaming at him to read to her because she told him that's what his teacher said she was supposed to do. She screeched how much the encyclopedias cost. She'd slap him and say he wasn't even trying. Why he couldn't read a word in any of the books. Not a word."

"It's a case of a parent not understanding." Jean sighed. "I know the teacher did not have encyclopedias in mind when she told Maurice's mother to get some books. Then what happened?"

"She beat him." Flo turned away so that Jean wouldn't see her crying. "He came to me all black and blue. Swollen eyes. I'll just never forget that little fellow pounding on my door. The worst of it is, Maurice took to her with a knife when he got free of the ropes that she had him tied up with. He stuck the knife in her arm. Just so angry inside. Fuming, raging anger is all he felt. I kept him with me for one full semester of school.

"I begged her to let me have him. I'd raise him right and see that he got the help he needed. Matter of fact, I have a daughter who's a teacher. Danielle offered to help me with him. So did my son. Donald used to come by and get Maurice and take him to the zoo and baseball games.

"Maurice was starting to act like a normal child. He was doing better in school. And then here she comes. Going to move to a nicer place she tells me. Going to take care of Maurice. She had another baby on the way so she decided to straighten herself out again. Patricia, that's her name, can get herself straightened out for about ten minutes. Then she backslides. It purely broke my heart when she took Maurice away from me. Wasn't a month and he's back here hiding from her.

63

"That's the way it's been for years. He'd be with me for a while. Maybe a week. Sometimes a month. Then the crazy pounding on the door with that lunatic on the other side. She'd haul Maurice out of here. He'd be with her until she beat him or left for a week or did some other crazy thing. Now I ask you, what chance has that boy had? Just tell me. What chance has that youngster had?"

"He said you put him out. Something about sniffing."

"That glue business. Now isn't that something. Letting that stuff eat up their noses and their brains. Can you even imagine sniffing glue! What's the world coming to. Me and my friends went all through school and never would have done such a thing. Even the wildest and craziest of the kids would never have done such a thing. We'd have got our little rears whipped until we couldn't sit down if we had done anything like that. My daddy took to my tail one time because my teacher told him I'd eaten a finger full of paste." Flo laughed. "I just keep wishing for the old days. So much about the old days was good."

Flo ran her open hand across the flowered pillow on the couch. "I told him I couldn't take that kind of behavior. If he was going to come back here high, he couldn't come back. That's all there was to it. Not one of my own children ever did things like that. I couldn't let Maurice do it. I truly believed, Jean. I truly in my heart believed that it would matter to him what I thought. That maybe I'd be more important to him than that glue. It didn't turn out that way. He kept it up. Then he got in all that trouble in school. He hit his principal. Lordy. Lordy in heaven that he could do such a thing. I was glad that

64

they sent him to Morton Hills. I figured maybe there was a chance that you people could do something with him. And now here this. Running away. I'm weary of it. I tell you surely as I sit here, I'm plain weary of it."

They both sat in silence for several minutes. The clock on the mantle ticked and chimed. Jean finally spoke. "Do you have any idea where he is now?"

"He did come home from Morton Hills. He called me to say he had done really well out there. He wanted to know if he could spend his furlough, as you people call it, with me. I told him that his visit would be as welcome as spring. Danielle and I met him at the bus stop within ten minutes after he got back into the city. We had a grand old time. I took him shopping and bought him two new shirts. We went to the movies. He was just doing fine. It sort of surprised me that he had stayed at Morton Hills as long as he did."

"Then what went wrong? Why didn't he come back?"

"If you want my opinion, I think it had something to do with that niece of the Bensons. She was visiting her cousin. Those Bensons are not the best people that you'd want to know, but they're not the worst. Mrs. Benson's niece, Carminetta, is a wild one. Maurice took a liking to her. He no sooner saw that girl, and he was down there making eyes at her and carrying on. And her with a baby and all. I told him he didn't need to be taking any interest in a child who had a child. That's what she was. Just a child and toting that baby around. She couldn't be any more than sixteen or seventeen.

"I knew he had to be out of here by three on Sunday to get back to Morton Hills by seven. I reminded him and I reminded him. He didn't pay any mind. About one o'clock on Sunday that Carminetta came strutting down here asking for Maurice. He'd like to have knocked me over getting to the door. Out he went and I haven't seen him since. As soon as you said who you were, I knew. I just knew he never made it back to Morton Hills."

"Have the police been here looking for him?"

"They've got a lot more to do than track down a fifteen-year-old boy who has run away from Morton Hills. Let him get in some serious trouble, though, and they'll be by hunting him down."

"I'm sure Maurice's social worker notified the police that he was a runaway."

"That doesn't matter. They'll get him when they have time."

"But you think this girl...what's her name?"

"Carminetta."

"You think she has something to do with his not returning?"

"I'm pretty sure that would be the case. Such a pretty girl. But she had that look about her. You know what I mean? Like she was grown up way beyond her years. Real wild hair. Makeup an inch thick. And those outfits she wears. Lordy. Lordy. In my day a girl would have been arrested for dressing like that."

"Do you think this Benson family would be willing to tell us how to get in touch with Carminetta?"

"They'd likely tell me, but there's not a doubt in mind that they wouldn't tell you a thing because you're..." Flo didn't

66

finish the sentence.

"White. Because I'm white."

"I didn't want to say that, but it's true. They'd probably think you were up to no good. Let me walk down there and see what I can find out. Would you mind waiting here?"

"I'll wait all day if we can get some lead on Maurice. I really want to help him, Flo. I want to help him even more after all you've told me. He has a lot of good in him. He acts so tough and...well, it's all a front with him. I think he just wants someone to love him and care about him."

"That I do."

"I'm not blaming you. You've worked a miracle keeping him out of even more trouble, but he has to pull his school work up or he won't go to school. If he's not in school, he doesn't have a lot of choices."

"The streets. That's it." Flo stood up to leave. "Pour yourself some more tea. I shouldn't be long."

Jean leaned comfortably back against the sofa while she waited. Her eyes never left the picture of the smiling Maurice, and her thoughts never stopped recalling what it must have been like for him when he was with his mother. Jean knew so little about Flo, yet she was grateful to the woman who treated Maurice with greater kindness than his own mother. Jean was still staring at the picture when she heard the footsteps of Flo coming up the stairs on the front porch.

She walked into the room and smacked her lips. "They must have asked me a hundred times if Carminetta was in some kind of trouble. They didn't want to tell me anything until I assured them that I was trying to keep Carminetta out of

67

trouble by keeping Maurice away from her. It seems the girl lives with her sister and her mother. They all stay at the grandmother's. The old woman is in some kind of nursing home or hospital. They didn't seem to know anything except that she lets her daughter and granddaughters live in her flat."

"Is it nearby?"

"It's in a bad neighborhood. Oh, these neighborhoods. When I was a girl you lived in a nice neighborhood even if you were poor. Now if they're poor, they got to tear the place apart and bring in those drugs. I'm sick to death of the drugs and what they're are doing to our children." She folded up the piece of paper that had Carminetta's address. "I think it's best that I go alone. Would you want to tell me how I can get hold of you? I'll call if I find out anything."

Jean took a notepad from her purse and wrote down her home and work numbers. "Would you mind giving me your number, also? I'll call you if we hear anything at Morton Hills about Maurice."

They walked to the door together. Flo had come to like the woman who seemed as worried about Maurice as she was worried herself. Flo linked arms with Jean, patting her hand to offer some comfort. "Maybe between the two of us we can pound some sense into that boy's head."

"We can hope."

"When you're dealing with the likes of Maurice, Jean, you got to do a lot more than hope."

CHAPTER SEVEN

Sometimes Flo forgot what it was like to live in homes where the noise never stopped and people entered and left their houses feeling fear. Fear that someone would break in while they were home, and fear that someone would hurt them if they left their homes.

She walked past house after house that had been splattered and marred with painted names and initials and gang threats. In dark entranceways and in abandoned stores and buildings, drugs and money were exchanged as an ordinary way of life. Litter filled the streets and dogs ran loose to poke through overturned garbage cans. Flo looked up from the paper that contained Carminetta's address. Although one of the numbers was missing from the two story building that sat near the corner, Flo knew that one of the flats in that building must be where Carminetta lived.

The hall to the second floor was dark and as covered with garbage and graffiti as the streets that Flo had passed. She could hear children crying and loud voices trying to scream the babies into silence. She knocked on the door. No one answered. Flo leaned her ear against the door. She was sure she heard an infant crying. Her hand went to the doorknob. Flo turned the knob and entered the flat. "Is anyone here?" Flo called out. "Is anyone home?"

The crying grew louder. Flo was afraid. She feared she might have walked into something dangerous. Her first thought was to get out, but she kept thinking about the baby's cry. She called out again. "Is anyone here?" Then she walked to the room where she'd heard the baby crying. "Oh, no." Flo sighed. Marvin was laying on the floor. He had fallen out of the crib. "Oh, you poor little thing." Flo scooped him up into her arms. His left eye was swollen. For an instant he stopped crying when Flo picked him up. He looked at her and began screaming again.

Flo went to the kitchen to find a bottle for the baby. She took a piece of ice from the refrigerator and wrapped it in a dishrag and it moved it gently back and forth on the infant's swollen eye. She was bent over the sink when suddenly the baby was grabbed from her arms. "What!" Flo spun around.

"What you doing here?" Loreen cuddled Marvin. "How'd you get in my house?"

"The door was open." Flo moved away from the girl's angry face. "I heard the baby crying. I found him on the floor. He's been hurt."

"Darn her." Loreen rubbed her face gently against the baby's. "That Carminetta left him. She's got no right to have a baby. Never treats him good or nothing Whatcha want with us?"

"I'm trying to find my nephew. Maurice. Maurice Davis."

Loreen held the baby with one arm and fixed him a bottle with her free hand. "He ain't here. He ain't been here in a couple of days."

"But he was here?'

"Yes, ma'am." Now that Loreen knew the woman meant her no harm, her manner softened. "He hangs out with that trashy sister of mine. Marvin's mama."

"Do you have any idea where I might find him now?"

"Probably out on them streets some place. How come you looking for him?"

"He's run away from Morton Hills. It's just a matter of time before the police pick him up. He might not be so lucky the next time. I mean they might send him some place that's not quite as nice as Morton Hills."

"How old is Maurice?"

"Fifteen."

Loreen broke out laughing. "Wait'll Miss Fancy Face finds that out. She keep calling him *her man*. Why she ain't got nothing but some boy. I knew he was a boy. The liar. He be telling us he was eighteen."

Flo watched the young girl handling the child. She was very gentle and very loving. "You're good with the child."

"Somebody's gotta be. It sure ain't Carminetta. My mama she works two jobs. She don't got time for nobody. I'm gunna kill that Carminetta what with her leaving Marvin all by hisself. He could've got hurt bad. Ain't it funny how some don't have no sense at all?" Loreen set Marvin down in the playpen.

"You're like a little mother."

"It ain't 'cause I wanna be. I got homework. I try to do real good in school. Not like Carminetta. Mama couldn't keep that girl in school no way. All Carminetta wants to do is run them streets and find some dude to buy her things. Like that Maurice. Ma'am, I'm tellin' you, Carminetta using that boy something awful."

"That's what I was afraid of. That's why I'm trying to find him. His teacher is looking for him, also. There are many

71

people who want to help him if he'd just take the help."

"I bet you love him. I can tell. You look like a nice lady."

"Can you tell me where he is?"

"Not for sure." Loreen lied. She couldn't bring herself to tell on a boy her own age. Given the choice of telling on him or lying to this stranger, Loreen preferred to lie. "But if I see him, I gunna tell him you was here looking for him. And I sure gunna tell Carminetta how old he is and that he's in trouble. Probably won't do you no good. Carminetta is in trouble herself half the time. I don't wanna be nothing like that girl. I got plans. Big plans for me. I'm gunna get outta here. You wait and see."

Flo admired the girl. As young as she was, she seemed to know that there was something better than what she had. "I'll bet you will. I'll just bet that you'll find a way out of here. Thank you for talking with me. You will be sure to tell Maurice that it's very important that I talk with him. You won't forget now, will you?"

"No, ma'am. I can be responsible. I ain't like my sister."

Loreen stood by the door as Flo turned to look at the baby. "He's a really adorable child. Put some ice on his eye. Wrap the ice in a paper towel and rub it gently by his eye. That baby shouldn't be left alone."

"I know, ma'am." Loreen went back into the living room and opened her math book to study. Her mind wandered as she tried to think just how much she would tell Carminetta of what she had learned about Maurice. She knew her sister well enough to know that if Carminetta knew the truth, she would tease and torment Maurice about his age and about being wanted by the police. Suddenly Loreen thought about the scrap of paper in her sister's dresser drawer. Maurice had written down his mother's address.

Loreen went into the bedroom and took out the piece of paper. She could barely make out the handwriting. It was like that of a child who had just learned to write. Loreen opened up the closet and took out a jacket for Marvin. "Come on, Tough Stuff, you and me is going to see if we can find Maurice."

Loreen ignored the young men on the corner who called out to her as she walked from the bus stop to the building where Maurice said he lived. The woman who answered the door was as Loreen expected her to be. She leaned against the door jam, barely able to speak. Then she screamed, "Maurice! Maurice. Get yourself here. Some girl..." Her voice trailed off. "He be here. Wait." She shut the door on Loreen.

Loreen sat on the top step waiting for Maurice. Where he lived was no different than where she lived. Loreen wondered why so many people were so poor.

Maurice opened the door a crack and peeked out. "It's you. I thought it was some of them cops or somebody I don't wanna see. Whatcha doin' here? Ain't nothin' wrong with Carminetta is there?"

"I ain't got no idea where Trash Face is. That ain't why I come here. Your auntie is lookin' for you."

"Oh." Maurice sat on the step with Loreen. "What she wantin'?" Maurice acted as if he were angry.

"She says she wants to help you. That teacher, too."

"PB? She stickin' her nose in my business now. Whew.

73

Ain't nobody gunna leave old Maurice alone."

Loreen smiled. "You ain't quite as *old* as you been telling us you is. Ain't that right?"

"My Auntie Flo been running her mouth to you?"

"I liked your Auntie Flo. She was real nice to me and Marvin. She found Marvin all by hisself. Trash Face left him alone. He could have got kilt or something. Your auntie was trying to help him."

"How Auntie Flo know about you and Carminetta?"

"Didn't ask."

"Them Bensons. They run their faces to Auntie Flo. I betcha that auntie of yours told my auntie all about Carminetta."

"So who cares." Loreen pulled Marvin closer to her. "It's cold in these here halls."

"Wait. I get us a blanket for the baby Marvin." Maurice ran into the apartment and came back with a red blanket that he tucked around the baby. His hand touched Loreen's leg as he wrapped the blanket around Marvin.

"Hey, boy. Don't be touching my knees or nothing." She shoved his hand away.

"Whatcha talkin' about? I just wrappin' up Marvin." Maurice smiled at the baby. "He sure is a cute dude. Looks real nice in them outfits I got him."

"Carminetta, too. She stand in front of that mirror or struts around like some kinda queen in all them duds you bought her. You is crazy spendin' all that money on Trash Face. You already in a pile of trouble. Whatcha want to get in more trouble over her for? She gunna dump you. I'm telling you, boy. Carminetta ain't got a good bone in her body."

"Why you keep sayin' that? Carminetta loves me. She told me so. She said I was the nicest man she ever know'd."

"Wanna know how many she's told that one to? About any man that ever come within ten feet of our house. Maurice, Carminetta ain't no good. Why can't you see that? She's my sister, but I know she ain't no good."

"Sometimes I think that sure be the truth. Other times Carminetta is real good to me. At first I thought she was kinda like Georgette. That's Ron's woman. Georgette is sweet and gentle. She don't never yell or nothin' at Ron."

"Who's Georgette?"

"She's my cottage parent at Morton Hills. I suppose my auntie she be tellin' you all about Morton Hills."

"She said you run away from there." Loreen looked at Maurice's sad face. "Is it real important that you have someone like Georgette?"

"I ain't got much. Havin' a real girlfriend would be special. Everybody be wantin' someone."

"Well, I can tell you, Caminetta ain't that girl. Nothing special about Trash Face."

"What about you, Loreen? You gotta a boyfriend?"

"I don't want one. I got my schooling. I ain't gunna get a boyfriend and have no babies. I told you that."

"You can have a boyfriend without havin' no babies."

"Yeah, a lot you know. Half the dudes at my school think they gunna be men by being daddies. Ain't nothing about being a daddy that makes you grown up. Every dog running them streets can be a mama or a daddy. Having puppies don't make none of them dogs grown up men and women."

"What you think makes a man a grown up?"

"Taking care of his family. Having a job. Lots of things, but just being a daddy ain't one of them. I don't take to them wall leaners and dudes hanging out on corners. Um. Um. Lazy no goods. I'm gunna get me an education. Then I'm gunna get me a job. When I get to be about twenty-five I might get married and have me a baby. You can see how Carminetta does. She ain't grown up. She ain't ready to take care of no baby. She likes to party. I guess I don't blame her none really. She should be having fun, but then she shouldn't had no baby if she wanted to have fun."

"You is like a grown lady already."

"What you mean?"

"You think like a grown person. You sound like some of them grown ups I hear talkin'. They says you should wait to have babies and you should get an education. I ain't very smart myself." Maurice looked down at a gum wrapper on the stairs. "If I tell you somethin' you won't laugh or nothin' at me?"

"Depends."

"Then I ain't tellin' you."

"Okay. I won't laugh."

"I can't read. Can't read a lick. I ain't braggin' or nothin'. I hate it 'cause I can't read. Peoples is always laughin' at me. That hurts. I mean it really hurts me when they make fun of me. I can't help it. I tried, and no matter how much I tried, I never could make no sense out of all them

76

letters. PB was helping me. She made me see how the letters made words. Some of it was startin' to make sense. You read?"

"Yeah. I read lots. I like books. I love readin' about all kinds of places in the world. Sometimes I think all those things I read about in the books couldn't really happen to people. Someday." Loreen looked at him. "You just wait, Maurice. Someday you're gunna hear about me being in one of them places. I'm gunna send you a card and tell you I'm in Florida. Or maybe even France. Who knows where I'll be."

"I can't read no card."

"You could if you'd go back to Morton Hills. You oughta just get yourself back there. You oughta do like your auntie and that teacher says. You ain't got no business messing around with Carminetta. Please, Maurice, won't you be doing like I ask? I'll be your friend. I'll care about you."

"How come you'd be doin' that?"

Loreen shrugged her shoulders. "I guess 'cause I think you're nice and I know Trash Face is gunna hurt you. That ain't right. It ain't right that someday you ain't gunna be able to read my card." Loreen smiled at him.

Maurice reached over and touched her hand. Loreen pulled away from him. "I don't mean I wanna be your girlfriend or nothing like that. I just wanna be your friend."

"Whatcha talkin' that way for? Ain't no way boys and girls is friends. Whoever heard 'bout somethin' like that?" Maurice dropped his hands to his knee.

"Sure I can be a friend. You can talk to me. You can call me. I'll listen to you, Maurice."

77

"And what should I be tellin' the other dudes that got women? Oh this here Loreen. She be my friend, but I don't touch her or nothin' like that. They'll laugh me right off the street."

Loreen smiled at him. "Then maybe you'll stay off them streets. You do this for me and Marvin. Make Marvin proud of you. Hey, I got an idea?" Loreen scooted around and faced him. "You be Marvin's uncle. I'll teach him that you is his uncle. That way you'll *have* to make him proud."

"I don't know. I got an uncle. He's sitting on time. Robbed a grocery store. He ain't no good."

"But you'll be a good uncle. I'll tell Marvin how you went back to Morton Hills and you learned how to read and you did all kinds of good things. Will you do it, Maurice? Will you do it for me and Marvin? Like we is your family. Me and Marvin and your Aunt Flo. You don't need that no good mama of yours and that Trash Face."

"Hey, don't you be talkin' about my mama."

"That's it, Maurice." Loreen's face turned red with anger. "Defend your mama even when she don't do right by you. You know you don't have to do that."

"I love my mama."

"What's your mama say about you goin' back to Morton Hills?"

"My mama she don't even remember I went there the first time around. She's out of it." Maurice laughed. "Sometimes I gotta remind my mama who I is. Ain't that somethin'? Mama don't even know me about half the time."

"Is you gunna do it for me and Marvin?" Loreen reached

over and touched Maurice's hand.

"How come you be touchin' me?"

"Friends can touch each other's hands. Ain't no harm in that."

"Wasn't you just the one grabbin all away and stuff like I was poison or somethin' bad? Now here you come touchin' my hand."

"I wanna be your friend, Maurice." Loreen patted his hand with the same type of gentleness that she touched Marvin. "So what's your answer?"

"What's Carminetta gunna say?"

Loreen laughed. "Probably ask you how much you got in your wallet before she says goodbye. Trash Face will have a new dude before you hit your hip on the doorknob on your way out."

Maurice took Marvin's fingers in his large hand. "You really think I can make somethin' of myself. Sorta be like one of them dudes you might want someday?"

Loreen couldn't bring herself to lie to him. "Maybe not like the kinda man I want, but you can do somethin' with your life. You don't have to hang out on them corners causing trouble and using that crack and other junk that's gunna fry your brains. You don't have to waste your life, Maurice. You just don't have to be a mess like some of them dudes."

"I guess I best be gettin' to my auntie's. She'll know what to do. Come on. I'll sees to it that you and Marvin get home. No tellin' who's crawlin' around them streets now."

"Ain't you gunna say goodbye to your mama?"

Maurice started down the steps. "That woman won't even

79

know that I'm outta here."

"What about the blanket?"

"Ain't no problem. Just take it. Can't be lettin' Marvin get cold or nothin' like that." Maurice stood at the bottom of the stairs holding the door open for Loreen. He watched her coming down the stairs. She held the baby close to her. He wondered why until tonight he hadn't thought that she was as pretty as Carminetta. "I sure do be wishin' you'd change your mind about me."

"I won't. I got too much to do with my life to be messin' with boys. Just too much to do. Ain't that right, Marvin?"

CHAPTER EIGHT

Maurice had many regrets about coming back to Morton Hills. He hated the squabbling that went on day and night with the other boys. They'd argue about who was sitting in a chair first. They fought over nothing and everything. When a moment of silence settled itself in a room, it was as if they couldn't stand the quiet. Someone would have to say something to anger someone else. Pop Mosley would take it as long as he could. Then his calm disappeared and he'd go after the troublemakers.

"If I had the money," he often roared out, "I'd buy about an hour of peace and quiet. Just one hour of not having to listen to the word *mama* and not hearing anyone carrying on like a nut because someone walked in front of them or got their booty near someone else's. I swear, living with you kids is like living with bombs that have been lit and are ready to go off."

Once Pop had his say, he'd wander off and sit with one of the boys to try to tell him how he could have handled a situation differently so that an argument could have been avoided. He seldom had to speak to Maurice, and that was what bothered Ron Mosley. Maurice stayed to himself. His size prevented most of the boys from starting trouble with him, but there were a few who didn't see Maurice as any more of a threat to them than the other smaller boys. Maurice, though, always chose to walk away from fights.

It wasn't Ron who discovered why Maurice chose to ignore the name calling and the challenges and dares. Georgette was the one who finally reached Maurice. She knew that Maurice had grown fond of her, and she made sure that Maurice had the chance to help her whenever he could. For months after Maurice was returned to Morton Hills he remained quiet, almost silent, around her. It was the letter from Loreen that opened the way for Georgette and Maurice to talk.

Georgette asked Maurice to help her move the washer and dryer so that she could clean under them. "I've never seen so much dirt. It always seems as if dirt can find a place to get to so that I can't get to it." Georgette knelt down to wipe up the lint and water stains that had collected on the floor under the washing machine. "Maurice, can you get me a sponge? Put some of that soap on it. The stuff sitting on the shelf up there."

Maurice reached for the soap and dribbled a few drops on the wet sponge. He handed the sponge to Georgette. Then he sat down on the floor where she was scrubbing. "I got me a problem."

"Is that so?" Georgette smiled. "Seems everyone here has a problem or they wouldn't be here, but what's yours, Maurice?"

"I got this here letter. Loreen done wrote me."

"Who's Loreen?"

Maurice thought a minute. He wasn't quite sure how to explain who Loreen was. "You see she's this here sister of Carminetta."

"And who's Carminetta?"

"They's sisters like I said. Carminetta she like to run the streets. Loreen's her sister and Loreen is tryin' to help me.

82

She says Carminetta ain't nothin' but some Trash Face."

Georgette laughed at the name. "A Trash Face, huh. It doesn't sound as if she's got much to offer."

"Loreen don't be likin' no punks or dudes who just hang out. Loreen, she want a good man."

"I can understand that. I don't know of too many women who don't want good men." She waited, knowing that sooner or later Maurice would explain his problem.

"Like I said. I got me a problem. Ron give me this here letter. I know'd it's from Loreen 'cause I can see her name on the envelope." He reached in his shirt pocket and took out the letter. "See." He pointed to the return address. "Loreen Cummings. That's what them letters say. Loreen Cummings." He tapped his fingers on the name.

"What did she say in her letter that's bothering you?"

"That's the problem I got. I can't read the letter. I don't want no one knowin' my business. Can you be readin' Loreen's letter to me?"

"Of course, Maurice." Georgette dried her hands on the rag that she had tucked into the waistband of her jeans. "You should have just asked. You know I'd be glad to do it." She took the letter that he held out to her. "Why look. It's a card." Georgette held it up so that he could see it.

There was an elephant and a mouse on the card. "It says, *Who says you can't be different and still be friends*."

"I don't get it."

"Well," Georgette studied the card for a minute. "It's like...Well, Maurice, an elephant and a mouse aren't anything alike. You often hear how a mouse can run up the trunk of an

83

elephant and stop it from breathing. The elephant dies because it can't breathe. I don't believe that. It's just kind of one of the tales that gets started and people go on believing it."

Maurice took the card and looked at it. "So's that what she be saying. A mouse can kill an elephant?"

"No." Georgette shook her head. She regretted trying to explain the tale that so many repeated about mice and elephants. "I think Loreen's message is that you and she are different, but that she's still your friend."

"Hm." Maurice opened the card. "See. Lookee here. She wrote somethin'." He handed the card back to Georgette.

Dear Maurice,

I am fine. Trash Face still running the streets. Marvin standing up and walking nearly. I got to be watching everything so as he don't pull stuff over on hisself. I seen your Auntie Flo. She and me have had lots of talks. We both really care about you. I know you ain't going to be coming home for a long time, but your Auntie Flo and me wants to come and see you. She said we could bring Marvin. Carminetta won't care. She gots herself a new boyfriend and she don't even ask nothing about you. I say this because I don't want you getting no hopes up about Carminetta. You just work on learning at Morton Hills. Auntie Flo and me is proud of Uncle Maurice. No matter what, you don't forget that we care about you and we want you to do real good. Don't forget that Loreen is your friend and I'll stand by you.

Love Loreen

"That's a really nice letter, Maurice. Loreen sounds like a nice girl. Are you going to write her back?"

"She be too nice. She don't have no use for dudes like me. But I think to myself that maybe I will be writin' her back even if she don't like me like no boyfriend or nothin' like that."

"That's not at all what she said. She said she was your friend. She said that she cared about you. She said she wanted to come and see you. How on earth can you believe that she has no use for you?"

Maurice picked up little pieces of lint from the floor. His hands worked the lint between his fingers. "I just ain't nobody, Georgette. Nobody that's gunna amount to nothin'. Now Loreen, she wanna a man who can...Heck, I don't know for sure just what that girl be wantin' but I sure know it ain't me. I just can't never get that off my mind. I sure be wantin' to be a man like she be wantin' and I don't know how."

"You're a good person, Maurice. You sure do a lot of things that you shouldn't do, but I've never seen anyone try harder than you're trying. Is it because Loreen wants to be friends and you want more than that? Maybe you'd like to have Loreen as a girlfriend?"

"Sure. Don't know no dude who don't be wantin' a lady of his own. That there Loreen, now she be havin' plans. She don't want no babies until she gets to be a lady. Loreen now she be talkin' about goin' to some of them places in those there books that she always be readin'. Them's big plans. And here I don't even read."

"You're learning. PB says that you're doing great in school. Pop and I are really pleased with your behavior in the cottage. You don't fight. You don't argue. In fact," Georgette looked him straight in the eye, "we were getting worried about you. We thought you might be depressed or something because you're so quiet and you stay by yourself far too much."

"I don't want no trouble. I gots one thing on my mind and that's gettin' out of this place. I wanna get to my Auntie Flo's and go to school like them other dudes. I wanna make Loreen proud of me. I wanna get to be like the kinda dude she be talkin' about. You didn't even know, but now I'm Marvin's uncle. I gotta be makin' somethin' of myself so that Marvin can look up to me."

"Ah," Georgette smiled. "So that's it. You're being this perfect kid for a reason. And a very good reason." She put her arm around him. "That makes me even prouder of you, Maurice."

He blushed from the compliment. "You think they maybe gunna shorten my time 'cause I doin' okay?"

"That I don't know." Georgette moved back on her knees to continue scrubbing the floor. "What you did was pretty serious. You're really lucky that you were sent back here instead of to one of those other places. If you hadn't been so young, you'd have ended up in jail for what you did. Selling drugs is nothing to sneeze at. That's heavy duty. If you had just run from here, well, that's not too serious. Lots of boys run. But it was the drug business that made it different. You've only been here about three months. You were sent here for a year to begin with. You add the new charges on top of that, well, I don't know. I have to be honest, Maurice. I can't see how you are going to be released from here in less than a year, and that's providing you continue behaving."

"Whew!" Maurice leaned against the washing machine. "Ain't no way I be lastin' no year. I be missin' them streets and my friends. I gotta be lookin' after Marvin and Loreen. I gotta be doin' so much stuff. Ain't no way, Georgette. Ain't no way they be keepin' me here no year and a half."

"No one is keeping you here, Maurice. There are no walls here. No locks. You have to keep *yourself* here. You have to want to stay and get the help. I think Loreen and your auntie would want that. You really can't do much to help take care of Marvin and Loreen if you don't get yourself together first."

"Sure ain't what I be wantin' for me." Maurice dipped his sponge in the bucket. "Sure ain't no way what I want. I wants out is what I want. Out. Out. Out."

Georgette felt the need to tell Jean what she had learned about Maurice. She was sure the information would help her. Perhaps together they could persuade Maurice to stay and to make an effort to learn. Georgette believed that if she and Jean kept reminding Maurice how important Loreen and Marvin were to his life, perhaps he would not run again. For their sake, as well as his own, Jean and Georgette kept telling Maurice that he should remain at Morton Hills until he was released.

Flo and Loreen's visits helped Maurice. His aunt didn't approve of what he asked, but finally went along with his telling everyone that she was his mother. Having a mother visit was important, and the tormenting that Maurice put up with because he was among the few whose mother had never

87

visited came to a stop. Maurice didn't deny the rumors that the boys spread. Almost everyone of the boys in the cottage believed that Loreen was Maurice's girlfriend and that Marvin was his son. Maurice wondered, as he saw the other boys staring at Loreen, what they would have thought if the even prettier Carminetta had shown up for a visit.

Once Maurice learned how to use a calendar, he made sure that each day was marked off and that he carefully wrote in the days that Flo and Loreen would be back to visit. Every night before he went to sleep, Maurice would place his head on the pillow so that he could see the calendar that hung on the wall next to his bed. Silently he would nod his head as he counted off the days until Flo and Loreen would return. For the first time in his life Maurice began to feel as if he belonged to someone and that people cared about him. He thought of the long bus trip that Flo and Loreen took just to spend a Sunday afternoon with him. He was sure they wouldn't do that unless he truly mattered to them.

Georgette was the first to notice that Maurice stopped talking about his mother and the things that he invented about her to make her sound as if she were the mother he wanted her to be. He no longer told stories of how she was sick in the hospital and that's why she hadn't visited him earlier. The lies about all the things that his mother bought him or how she took him out to eat in expensive restaurants or on an airplane to New York were no longer part of the stories that Maurice created so that his life would seem normal. He even confessed to the other boys that Flo was not even his aunt, much less his mother. Reality was becoming more important to him than the lies he made up. He was sure that no one had ever been happier than he was when he finally was able to read Loreen's cards without Georgette's help.

More than anything Maurice wanted to go home for Marvin's first birthday, but it would be eight more weeks before Maurice would be given his first furlough. That meant he would have to go through most of summer school before he could look forward to the bus ride that would take him back into the city. Jean picked out a birthday card for him to send to the child that he had grown so fond of. Maurice struggled with each word that he wrote to the little boy. He told Marvin how when he grew up he would take him places, and that Marvin should be good and do just what his mother and Loreen told him to do.

Even though Maurice was not allowed to return home on furloughs, the summer was not as long as he thought it would be. Like most of the boys at Morton Hills, Maurice had come to love the outdoors. School didn't seem as bad or boring when he could lay on a bed of leaves that covered the forest floor and look up at the sky while he listened to Jean explain the world to him.

Jean loved the outdoors as much as the boys. On the day that was to end the summer session, Jean tramped with them through the forest. She called out, "Here you go, guys." She waved the paper in the air that she had brought with her. Then Jean handed out the paper and pens to the boys who had come to sit along the river's edge. "Today we're going to tackle some poetry. I don't want any of this 'PB how do you spell such and such.' I want these poems to be *your* poems. That means you use words that you can spell. Got it."

"I ain't gunna be writin' no poetry." Lionel threw his paper down on the ground. "That's sissy stuff."

"Suit yourself, Lionel. No one said you had to write a poem. That's the assignment today. Stare into space for all I care. Then I'll leave a space in my grade book where your grade is supposed to go. How does that grab you, Lionel?"

Lionel picked up the paper. "See. Lookee here what you made me do." He held up the paper that was smudged with dirt.

"Write a poem about dirt, Lionel. Or better yet, write a poem about a boy who threw his paper on the ground, how it got dirty, and then how he blamed someone else. You can call the poem *Dumping*."

"I ain't dumpin' on no one."

"Hey, man," Daniel interrupted, "no one wants to be listening to you runnin' that mouth of yours."

"Your mama."

"Your mama back." Daniel growled. "PB, why don't you drown him? He's useless."

Jean wondered if Lionel would ever quit blaming others for his problems. "The both of you better button up." She glanced at her watch. "You have forty minutes. And no asking each other how to spell a word. If you don't know, there's a good chance the one next to you doesn't know either. Just write."

She looked at them as they bent their heads over. Some of them began to write immediately. A few stared off beyond the hill as if the air would give them some idea as to what they should write about. Twice Lionel stood up and walked over to where she sat to tell her he couldn't think of anything about which to write. She shook her head and pointed to where Lionel had been sitting. "Sit, Lionel. Sit and wait for an idea."

Lionel walked back and flopped down. "This here stuff is stupid. Real stupid."

Jean could see that Maurice struggled with every word. He'd look up and close his eyes trying to remember what a word looked like so that he could write it down. Several times she saw him draw his pen back and forth through a word, scratching it out only to choose another that he couldn't spell.

At the end of the forty minutes Jean called out, "Okay. Time has run out. Bring me your works of art."

Mason handed her his paper. "It ain't no good. I couldn't figure out no way to say what I wanna say."

"You mean you couldn't think of a poem?"

"No. I thought of plenty. I knew all kinds of stuff to say. I don't know nothin' about spellin' them words."

"A prisoner of words."

"Whatcha talkin' about?"

"If you can't spell a word, Mason, you can't use the word. That means that you can't put your thoughts down on paper or you can't answer a question even if you know the answer, and all because you can't spell. It's like being a prisoner. You see what I mean?"

Mason shrugged and walked back to his place under a tree. Jean read through the poems. The boys laughed at some of them. Then grew silent, depending on the words she was

91

reading. "Here's Maurice's. Are you ready?"

"Yeah, PB, let's hear what Uncle Maurice got to say."

Jean pushed her glasses up on her nose. Then waited for the boys to get settled and silent. "The title is *The Other Side of the Sun*." Then she began reading.

"One day I going to the other side of the sun.
One day I be seeing just what is there
On the other side of the sun.
No drugs and hurt and no noise and pain
On the other side of the sun.
I can read and write on the other side of the sun.
Everything is clean and bright.
All the mamas love their children
On the other side of the sun.
Your daddy takes you fishing and no man hurts another.
Mamas hold their babies and life is good
On the other side of the sun."

Jean let out a deep sigh. Tears fell down her face. "That's a pretty neat poem, Maurice. I can't recall reading such a beautiful poem. In all the books of poetry I've read by the most famous people in all the world, I don't think I've ever read anything so beautiful."

"What's that dude talkin' about? Keep on writin' about that sun. Ain't nobody carin' about the sun." Lionel called out.

"Well, suppose you guys tell me. What do you think Maurice is trying to say? Otis?"

"Got me."

"Martin, what did the poem mean to you?"

92

"Sounds stupid to me. Ain't no one goin' to the other side of the sun. Even I know that and I don't know nothin'.'"

"Jeff." Jean looked from face to face hoping that someone would see what she knew Maurice was trying to say.

Jeff looked up at the sun. Then he answered. "See Maurice don't know nothin' about the other side of the sun neither. He sure knows about *this* side of the sun. I think Maurice, well, he's sort of fed up with what he sees. Like nothin' ain't right here. Drugs everywhere. Peoples don't be havin' much and mamas ain't always takin' care of their kids. I think Maurice kinda hopes if he could get to the other side of the sun, why things wouldn't be like they is here. Everythin' be good on the other side of the sun. That's what I be thinkin' Maurice writin' about in his poem."

"Is that what you meant, Maurice? Did Jeff understand your poem?"

"Yes, ma'am." Maurice hung his head. He wasn't sure if he liked being the center of attention.

"That's what poetry is, boys. It's just a way of writing your feelings. Sometimes you use symbols. To Maurice the other side of the sun is a symbol for a better life."

"No one exceptin' Jeff knew what I wanna say." Maurice sounded hurt.

"I did." Jean assured him. "I think some of the others did, also. But that's another thing about poetry, or really, anything that people write about. Each person who reads what has been written gets different things out of it. Readers always take something to what they are reading. The thing they are taking is themselves. They are taking all their experi-

93

ences. Sort of everything that has happened to them. It's their experiences and their beliefs and feelings that cause each person to come away with a different idea as to what the writer or poet was trying to say. In this case, Maurice, Jeff might have had some of the same experiences and hopes that you've had. That's why he understood."

"How come you understood, PB? You ain't never had no life like mine."

Jean looked at him and had a few instant thoughts about her own horrible childhood. "You'll never know that will you, Maurice?" She stood up. "I think that's a day for us, guys. If I'm not mistaken the coach has some relay races planned for you this afternoon."

Maurice walked along beside Jean. "Can I be gettin' my poem back? I wanna show Loreen. Maybe she not be thinkin' I so stupid if she see what I wrote."

"Sure, Maurice. But you know what I'd like for you to do?"

"What?"

"Copy the poem. I'd like to keep a copy. You can give the original to Loreen, but would you mind making a copy for me?"

His face glowed with a big smile. "You mean that? You mean you be wantin' a copy of my poem to keep forever?"

"Forever." She took his hand and held it as they walked up toward his cottage. Jean looked up at the beams of sun shining through the trees. "You know what, Maurice, you've started me wondering just exactly what is on the other side of the sun."

CHAPTER NINE

Jean was standing at the window of her classroom when she saw Maurice running across the field toward her room. He was waving his yellow paper. The very important yellow paper that had been signed by the superintendent at Morton Hills, the principal, and Maurice's social worker. The yellow paper that would release Maurice from the custody of Morton Hills. Jean waved to him through the open window. She wondered how a year could have passed so quickly.

"I gots them." Maurice held the yellow sheet high above his head. "Free. They done set me free."

Jean laughed. "You make it sound like you've been a slave."

"I was a slave. Little old diddle money they be givin' you for workin' in that hot old kitchen." He grinned. "I be goin' home now."

"You deserve it. You've done very well. I'm really proud of you. Are you going to come in and say goodbye to your friends?"

Maurice wrapped his fingers around the glass window panel that hung out over the ledge of the building. He kept moving nervously from foot to foot as he talked. "Ain't got no time. I gots to be seein' my social worker. Gotta get my gear ready. Gotta go see the superintendent and tell him what a good boy I gunna be. You know all that stuff."

"Sure, I know it, Maurice. I've seen a lot of you go out of here. The problem is, I've seen a lot of you come back. But I know, I surely know, that you're not going to be one of them."

"You about as right as you can be. Ain't no way I wanna be comin' back here." Maurice reached into his pocket. "Got somethin' for you." He held up two candy bars. "These is for you."

Jean reached out through the window and took the candy bars. They were melted beneath their wrappers. "I should be giving you a going away present instead of the other way around."

"They ain't no goin' away present or nothin. I stole a candy bar from you a long time back."

"You did?" Jean frowned. "Why here I thought you liked me."

"I be talkin' about a long time ago when I was ornery. Remember?"

"Yes." Jean smiled at him. "I remember when you were ornery."

"Before I even pulled your hair out. You talkin' to Mr. Krueger. I was slick as all get out. I had my hand in and out of that purse of yours. Thought I'd be gettin' your wallet until I seen that candy bar. Sorry. Real sorry."

"Your apology is accepted. Besides, it looks as if I'm coming out ahead on the deal. I'm getting an extra one back."

"You been real nice to me, PB. I gunna try real hard in school 'cause I want to make you proud of me."

Jean put her hand out the window and touched his face. "I know I'll have good reason to be proud. Now you have my home phone number in case you need me for anything. I mean it, Maurice. I want you to call me if you have any problems in school. Your Auntie Flo promised to keep in touch, also."

"Ain't gunna be no problems. I'm cool. Real cool."
He waved and raced across the field toward the main office.

Jean turned away from the window as she didn't want to
see him go. She walked to her desk and put the candy bars
next to the copy of the poem Maurice had written. Then she
opened up her file cabinet and took out Maurice's folder. The
note from the social worker said that the assignment to
Kennedy High School had been completed. Jean sighed and
shook her head in disgust. No matter how far Maurice had
come over the last year, Jean knew he would not survive in
regular high school classes. She had done all she could to
plead Maurice's cause. Jean had tried to get him assigned to a
vocational school, or at least to some school that had special
education classes.

Maurice himself had fought her on going to special
education classes. He had sat with his social worker and Jean
and argued that he would not go to school if Jean were going
to have him put in special education classes. Mrs. Mullins, his
social worker, believed he'd be better off going to Kennedy
High and struggling than not going to school at all.

When Maurice left the meeting to return to his cottage,
Jean continued to argue with Mrs. Mullins. "I know you think
he's right about going to regular classes. I know you honestly
believe that he won't go to school at all if he's put in special ed
classes, but I think if we put our foot down and tell him it's
special ed classes or he doesn't leave here, he'd change his
mind."

"We can't lie to him. He's been released. I don't have

much choice. If you get right down to it, Maurice is old enough to quit school. Don't you think Kennedy High is better for him?"

"No, I don't. He won't make it. He doesn't stand a prayer of lasting a month. Maybe not even a week. I've got his reading level way up, but not up to what will be expected at Kennedy. He'll be in regular classes with teachers who simply don't know how to work with kids like Maurice. I'd be willing to bet he won't be able to read the titles on the books they give him let alone be able to read what's in them. Maurice has a pretty short fuse. The first time someone makes fun of him, he's going off on them."

"You know what, I'm not even arguing with you. You're probably right. I don't think he's going to make it in a regular high school, either."

"Then why!" Jean yelled. "Why are we sending him to Kennedy and not to a school that has special ed classes?"

"It's his choice."

"His choice! Maurice hasn't made a half dozen good choices in his entire life. Why should we let him make a choice when we know better?"

"Sooner or later we have to turn loose of these kids and let them make some choices. They can learn something from poor choices."

"Can't we all. What we're probably going to learn is that Maurice is going down the tube in one hell of a hurry. Right down the tube. I can't believe with his record and with his background that you can sit there and say we ought to let him make the choice."

"My experience has been that when you let them make their own choices, they try harder."

"No matter how hard he tries, it won't be hard enough to pull him through regular high school classes."

"Part of the problem gets dumped at your doorstep. You were the one who brought his reading up. He didn't do all that bad on his test scores. He scored too high for classes for the mentally handicapped. I suppose we could have tried to put him in some kind of classes for the learning disabled."

"Sure we could have. Or the emotionally disturbed. But, of course, that wasn't his choice." Jean pitched a pencil across the room. "There's no sense arguing. We have different points of view. Normally I love different points of view. In Maurice's case, we should have made it clear to him that the decision was not his."

Mrs. Mullins argued in her own defense. "We're not talking about some little kid anymore. Maurice was a little over fifteen when he came here. He's going to be seventeen before long. Now you try and tell me how we can tell him he can't make decisions about himself."

Mrs. Mullins picked up Maurice's file and put it in her briefcase. "You've probably seen the last of Maurice. He won't be coming back here with the next offense. The courts will move him right along to the big time places. I doubt very much that any dust is going to collect on Maurice's file, and as his caseworker, I'll have him until I die or he turns eighteen."

"Or he dies."

"With some of these kids, we know that's a possibility. It's tough racket we're in. I sometimes wish I sold shoes."

Jean laughed. "I've done that. On my salary I had to work in the summer to earn enough to live on. For two summers I sold shoes."

"Consider yourself lucky. I still wait tables on the weekends. Sorry I wasn't the support that you wanted me to be."

"I'm sorry I blew my lid. We're both just doing our jobs the best that we know how to do them. Maurice had become sort of special to me. More than anything, I want Maurice to make it."

"Like the saying goes, it's not over until the fat lady sings."

"I don't like to sound totally hopeless, but on the day that Maurice goes through the gates at Morton Hills, I have this horrible feeling that the fat lady just walked on stage."

Jean was thinking about what she said to Mrs. Mullins as she put Maurice's file back in the cabinet. She looked up toward the superintendent's office, knowing that Maurice probably was sitting in that office as she stood at the window. *Please.* Jean looked up at the early afternoon sun. *Please let him be one of the ones who makes it.*

CHAPTER TEN

Flo didn't like the idea that Maurice had three weeks until school started. If Maurice had any hope of staying out of trouble until that time, Flo believed the hope lay with Loreen. As much as she wanted to help Maurice and Flo, Loreen would not give up the job that one of her teachers had helped her get.

"I wished I could do like you ask me, Auntie Flo, but I got a chance to make me some money. Besides, I can't be following Maurice around all day making sure he's not running them streets."

"I know, honey." Flo felt guilty for having asked. She had become as fond of the young girl as she was of Maurice. "It was wrong of me to ask. I've tried to get him interested in some of those programs at the park. They have baseball and track, and all sorts of things. They even have those cleanup projects for the city. It's not like those kids get a lot of money for their work, but it does give them a chance to get some experience. What with Maurice's record, I had to be truthful when I asked about getting him on one of the projects. The man at city hall who runs that program wasn't overjoyed about hiring Maurice."

"I told that Maurice that he better be getting it together. I know for a fact them there rap sheets follows as close behind you as a dog after a pork chop. It's like he's got a bad reputation and people who been straight don't be wanting nothing to do with him."

"It just purely makes me sick thinking that he's going to get himself in some kind of mess what with so much time on his hands. I'd have preferred it if they had kept him at Morton Hills until it was time for him to start school."

"You know, Auntie Flo, I been thinking. Suppose Maurice takes on the job of watching Marvin? Carminetta ain't no way gunna look after that boy. About half the time I come home and find him alone. I be worrying to death about little Marvin. Mama can't be watchin' him. She's just wore out from working. Maurice is crazy about that little Marvin. You think Maurice might take to the idea?"

"You know that's a thought. Perhaps if he had the responsibility of keeping the baby safe and...well, sort of protecting him." Flo pointed a finger at Loreen. "You know what? You just might be right." Her face brightened. "You might be exactly right."

"Then should we be fixing to ask him?"

"I think you might be able to convince him better than I." Flo didn't like excusing herself from responsibility, but she knew enough about young people to know that Maurice was more likely to listen to Loreen.

"That ain't no problem."

The care of Marvin was the first thing that Loreen talked about with Maurice when she saw him that night. He had only been home three days and each night he came to see Loreen. There was still a part of him that hoped Carminetta might be home, but when she wasn't, the disappointment faded quickly as soon as he started talking to Loreen.

"Whatcha mean, Loreen? Is I supposed to be his daddy or somethin'?"

"I told you, Maurice. You can be like his uncle. This Little

Tough Stuff don't have nobody to look out for him. Mama is working night and day. Trash Face in and out of here like lightning on a stormy day. My Marvin got messy pants and everything when I get home. Them welfare people find out what's going on here, and Marvin be gone in a flash and be in some kinda foster home."

"I don't know nothin' about takin' care of messy pants."

"You learned to read. You can be learning about messy pants a lot faster. Besides, messy pants ain't all there is to it. You can be taking Marvin to the park. Here you be writing me them letters saying how you gunna be looking after Marvin and all that. So, Big Mouth, now you oughta be doing what you be saying you gunna do."

Maurice thought back on the letters he had written to Loreen and Marvin. What she said was true. He had made promises to do what he could to help her and Marvin. "What the heck." Maurice grinned. "If Marvin not be carin' then I don't care."

With the agreement made, each morning Maurice met Loreen at the bus stop. She would hand him a bag filled with diapers and clean clothes. Then she boarded the bus for work, waving at Maurice as he stood there holding Marvin.

The promise that Maurice made to watch the child turned out to have many moments of pleasure. Fastening him in the swing at the park and watching Marvin's laughing face, always made Maurice laugh. Maurice also found joy in the fact that Marvin was the perfect one to listen to his troubles. No matter what Maurice said about the unfairness of life, or the feelings he had inside of him, Marvin only smiled and said nothing. Marvin responded to Maurice's sometimes anger by babbling and murmuring sounds that had no meaning.

There were many days, though, when Maurice wished more than anything that he had made no promise to Loreen about looking after Marvin. No matter where Maurice wanted to go, his days had to be planned around the small child's needs. His phone calls were interrupted by the child's cries of hunger or by a dangerous situation that Marvin had toddled into and from which Maurice had to save the boy. At the end of the day Maurice's arms were tired from carrying the child. By the end of the second week of watching the young boy, Maurice knew that caring for a child was not what he wanted to do. It was easy for Maurice to see why Carminetta left her son alone so often.

Maurice pleaded with Loreen to release him from his promise. Loreen pleaded back, making Maurice feel guilty by saying that if he loved Marvin, he would want to make sure that nothing happened to him.

Maurice welcomed Carminetta's advice that went against what Loreen believed. "That girl be worryin' all the time about that child. I leave him plenty of times and he be doin' just fine. Just be sittin' him in his playpen or crib. He ain't goin' no place. He be right there when you get back."

"How come you don't be lookin' after Marvin none? You's his mama. Shouldn't no way be up to me and Loreen to be lookin' after him. You gotta get off them there streets and be takin' care of Marvin."

"That so." Carminetta smoothed out her dress and slipped

on her heels. "So who's been puttin' you in charge of my life?" She walked out the door, leaving Maurice and the child by themselves.

Maurice paced back and forth thinking that Carminetta was right. Perhaps Marvin could be left alone without harm coming to him. Such thoughts didn't keep him from being angry with Carminetta because she could so easily walk out the door and leave the care of Marvin up to him.

Maurice watched Marvin take a step and tumble down before he pulled himself up and took another step. "You ain't no Tough Stuff. You be a pest. You hear me, Marvin. You be like a pest hangin' round my neck." Maurice picked him up and put him in his playpen. Marvin started screaming. "You quiet yourself, boy. You hear me. You quiet yourself. Uncle Maurice got things to do and places to go. He ain't gotta be lookin' after you every second of his day. You got that, boy."

Maurice walked out the door and down the steps onto the street. He had only gone two blocks when he turned around and headed back toward the apartment. Marvin was laying in the playpen. His unhappy eyes stared up at the ceiling. When he heard the door open, Marvin pulled himself up and reached out for Maurice. "Okay, Tough Stuff. You be comin' with Uncle Maurice."

Maurice ignored the remarks made to him as he passed by some of the young men that had once been Maurice's friends. He tried to make jokes with those who were teasing him. He waved back and yelled, "Why this here thing ain't mine. I done kidnapped him and I sellin' him for some bags." Maurice kept walking and trying to smile. He turned down

Taylor Street and walked into the neighborhood that he knew so well. He heard a familiar voice call out to him.

"Hey, Big Mo. What's going down, man?"

Maurice turned around and saw Hoagy standing in a doorway. "Hey, man." Maurice stopped and shifted Marvin to his other arm. "You be lookin' bad, Hoagy. Real bad. What's with you?"

"Turning some business. What's with the kid?"

"He be Carminetta's. You know that chick?"

"Who don't know her. Yeah. I know Carminetta."

"I be helpin' her sister Loreen. You know her?"

"Yeah. I seen her around. She thinks she's something. I'd like to bust her one. That Loreen looks at you like you is dirt."

Maurice wanted to defend Loreen, but he didn't want to argue with Hoagy for fear Hoagy would think he thought more of Loreen than he thought of Hoagy's opinion. "She be workin' some place and so I be takin' Tough Stuff out for some air. Showin' him around these here streets."

"You interested in some business?"

"No, man. I workin' at keepin' clean. Next time I be gettin' caught I gunna be sittin' on more time than I wanna be handlin'."

"Hey, listen, Big Mo, this is some easy money. You got the best coverup I ever seen. Not a chance of your getting hassled by the police or anyone else."

"Whatcha talkin' about?"

"The little dude. Let the little dude carry the stuff."

"Whatcha crazy or somethin'! I ain't messin' with no

stuff as long as I gots Marvin with me."

"We're talking some quick cash. Real quick. Buy the kid some duds. Give Carminetta somethin' nice. You know how she likes them nice flashy clothes."

"Me and Carminetta ain't nothin'." Maurice was thinking about having money in his pockets again. "Where's the action?"

"So you're interested?"

"I ain't sayin' for sure. Depends."

"A drop downtown. Can't take you more than an hour to make your rounds. Get this. A lawyer's office. Interested?"

"One trip. No more."

"One trip. It'll save me some time. " Hoagy entered the building and Maurice followed him up the dark hallway. "I appreciate your interest. I got a big one going down this afternoon. I don't have no time for this little stuff anymore." Hoagy handed the drugs to Maurice along with the address. "This guy don't want you in the building. You go to a pay phone and call this number. He'll meet you on the corner of Olive and Tenth. Tell him you're the guy with the baby." Hoagy laughed. "That oughta be a new trip for him. Buying from a baby."

Maurice tucked the drugs into Marvin's diaper. "Listen, Tough Stuff, I know'd I shouldn't be doin' this, but I gots a chance to make a deal. One deal and that's it." He kissed Marvin on the cheek. "You and me, we is buddies, huh, kid."

Maurice did as Hoagy said. He dropped the coins in the phone and asked for extension 128. In a low tone Maurice said, "I'm your man. By the phone on the corner. I gots a baby. You be knowin' me." Then he hung up and waited.

In a few minutes a well-dressed man came toward him. He put his hand on Marvin's back and patted him. He whispered, "You, scum. Using a baby like this." He flicked his hand open to show the money. Maurice put his hand up on Marvin's shoulder and took the money. Then he reached into Marvin's diaper and pulled out the drugs. As Maurice turned to leave, the man called out, "Oh, son. Just a minute."

Maurice looked at the man's face. He was angry. Maurice backed away. He didn't want any trouble. He didn't want anything to happen that would bring the police. "Yes, sir."

The man moved his face up close to Maurice's. "Look down, you dumb punk. Someone's been doing something with this."

Maurice looked at the packet the man held. The edges had been torn and the plastic bag was only half full. "I ain't done nothin' with it. You get what you pay for." Maurice turned around and jumped on the bus that had just stopped.

Maurice dropped the coins in the box, nodded to the driver, and took a seat at the back of the bus. He set Marvin on the seat next to him. "You be stayin' put, Tough Stuff." Marvin reached into his pocket and counted out the money. It was the amount that Hoagy said it would be. Maurice took those bills that now belonged to him and placed them in his shirt pocket, and he put the money that belonged to Hoagy in his pants' pocket. "Easy money, Marvin. Real easy money."

That night Maurice was asleep when he felt Flo shaking him awake. "Maurice. Maurice." She screamed at him. "What did you do to Marvin? Answer me, boy, what did you do to that child?"

"Huh?" Maurice sat up in bed. He could see the outline of his aunt as she stood above his bed in the darkened room. He rubbed his eyes and stretched. "Whatcha takin' about?"

"Loreen is at the hospital. She called from the emergency room. They had to pump that baby's stomach. He went into convulsions. What did you do to that child? Answer me," she screamed. "You tell me what you did to that poor little baby."

Maurice shot up in bed. "Marvin ain't dead. My Marvin ain't dead is he?"

"No. He's not dead. He's seriously ill. Oh, my lord." Flo sat down in a chair. "I can't believe you'd do anything to hurt that boy." She put her head into the palms of her hands. "I beg of you, Maurice, tell me you didn't hurt that baby."

Maurice couldn't stand to see her cry. Nor could he stand the thought of what she would do if he revealed what he thought had probably happened. Somehow Marvin had chewed through one of the bags containing the drugs. "You sure Marvin ain't gunna die or nothin'. You real sure."

"The poor little thing. That innocent little child. Loreen says the nurse blamed her. The woman accused Loreen of giving the baby drugs. Loreen was so upset she could hardly talk. Her mother left work to come and get her. They had to leave Marvin at the hospital. It happened right after you dropped Marvin off. Carminetta said Marvin was twisting and acting crazy. Then he went into convulsions. Please, Maurice, I have to know."

Maurice walked over to the window. He pulled the curtain back so that he could look out on the street. "I don't know nothin' about what you be sayin', Auntie Flo. I bet you anythin' Carminetta done somethin'. Might even be one of them crazy dudes she be bringin' up to her place." Maurice moved over to where his Aunt Flo sat. "I be more sorry than anybody if anythin' happen to Marvin. I loves that boy. You know that."

"Yes. I know." Flo's voice trailed off to a whisper. She felt relief that Maurice had not been involved. "I'm sorry, son. I guess I should have thought about it being Carminetta or that low life she travels with." Flo reached up to touch Maurice's hand. "We'll go to the hospital in the morning. Lord knows where those people are going to get the money to pay the bill." She stood up and let out a deep sigh. "I guess when it's a child's life, money doesn't matter, does it?"

"No, ma'am." Maurice returned to bed when she left the room. He buried his head in the pillow and cried and prayed that Marvin would be all right.

Carminetta and her mother were sitting next to Marvin's crib when Flo and Maurice arrived at the hospital. Maurice could not bring himself to look at Marvin more than one time. There were tubes in the child's nose and his little arms were fastened to needles that were attached to more tubes. Maurice only glanced at him. Then he ran from the room.

Maurice was leaning against a wall near the elevator when Loreen stepped off. She glared at him. "You is less than nothin', Maurice."

"Why come you be sayin' that about me, Loreen?" Tears fell from his eyes.

"Your Auntie Flo called me this morning. Here you be

110

talking about how you think Carminetta or one of her dudes done this. Maybe you can be getting away with your lies with Auntie Flo, but I ain't so dumb and foolish. Trashy as Carminetta is, she ain't that low down. I gotta believe her. She don't know nothing about any of this here problem with Marvin. You done something, Maurice. You done something to hurt that baby of mine. You is so low if I got below the dirt I still be looking down at you."

"I loves Marvin."

"Talkin' about love don't count for nothing when you hurt someone. Specially a little baby. You ain't gunna be his uncle no more. You come around to see me or my Marvin, and I gunna fix you good. I mean real good."

Maurice couldn't look at her, nor could he go on lying to her. "You gunna tell my Auntie Flo?"

Loreen barely whispered, "No, Maurice, I ain't gunna be telling her. Not because of you, Dirt Face. It ain't got nothing to do with my wanting to be protecting you. I just can't hurt her no more than she's been hurt. I think about that baby having Trash Face for a mama and you for an uncle. Whew! Ain't no baby in the world deserve you two." Loreen turned and walked away from Maurice.

The air on the street was still and hot. Maurice walked along kicking at the paper that blew along the sidewalk. He stopped in front of a store window. Behind the glass were radios and stereos and so many of the things that Maurice valued and wanted. His hand squeezed the bills that he had in his pocket from the delivery that he had made. Then he looked at the largest of the radios in the display. He wanted to

111

feel good because he knew how to get the money to buy the radio. Maurice felt only emptiness and loneliness.

For several minutes he stared at himself in the window. *Maurice, you so dumb. You always gotta be messin' up.* The man in the store stepped to the door to ask Maurice if he wanted any help in making a selection. "Ain't nobody gunna help me no more." Maurice turned and ran down the street.

CHAPTER ELEVEN

Louis sat across the table from Maurice. They had been in the study room for fifteen minutes and Maurice had not yet opened his book. Twice Louis had asked Maurice if he had any intention of studying the pages their teacher had assigned him. The first time that Louis asked, Maurice moved his elbow toward the book and pushed it onto the floor. The second time Louis asked, Maurice put his head down on his folded arms and acted as if he were going to sleep.

"Listen, Big Mo," Louis spoke in a low, impatient tone, "it doesn't matter to me whether or not you study. I'm going to get paid even if you flunk the test."

Maurice sat up. "You mean, man, they's paying you! "

"Yeah. You didn't know that."

"Why come you gettin' money and you just some dumb kid like me? Nobody ain't payin' me to learn nothin'."

There wasn't one thing about Maurice that Louis liked. "I'm a tutor. Every year the school hires ten students to help other students. I guess my luck ran out when they shoved you on me. I don't expect I'll be stuck with you too long. When Mr. Bradley wants to know how you're doing and I tell him you sleep, they're going to give me another student to work with. Someone who wants to learn."

"A big rat, huh? Runnin' your face to them there teachers."

"Listen, Mo, I don't owe you anything. You can sit there like a brick as far as I'm concerned. It doesn't matter to me whether you pass or whether they throw you out of this place. About all you want to do is cause trouble anyhow."

"You such a great big pet they oughta be puttin' you in a zoo." Maurice looked at the stocky boy who sat across from him. Maurice envied him that he was smart enough to tutor other students. "That's all junk in them books. Ain't none of them gunna help me get no job."

"Well, try getting a job without a high school diploma. You'll see how the *junk* helps you." Louis opened one of his own books. "I'm not here to argue with you. When you're ready let me know." Louis started making notes on a pad of paper.

"Whatcha writin' on the paper?"

"I'm outlining a chapter."

Maurice watched Louis' eyes move quickly across and down the pages in the book. Then he wrote several lines on the yellow paper. Maurice couldn't imagine how the boy could read and write so fast. "You be knowin' what all them words is?"

Louis kept on writing. "Not all of them. That's why I look some of them up in the dictionary. Or I go back and reread some of the stuff because I didn't get what the words meant."

"You always been smart in the head?"

Louis shrugged. "I like school if that's what you mean."

"You be like Loreen. She be tellin' me how she like school. She like puttin' her nose in them books."

"Loreen?" Louis thought about the girl in his English class. "Loreen Cummings?"

"Yeah. Loreen Cummings. She be Carminetta's sister."

Louis made a real effort not to smile. "You're a friend of

114

Loreen's?" Last semester Louis had tried two or three times to bring himself to ask Loreen out. Every time he came near her, he found he couldn't work up the courage to talk to her.

"I know'd her, but she ain't got a good word to say about me no more." Maurice stared out the window, thinking how much he missed being a part of her life. "I really messed up with Loreen. She done tried to be my friend, but I surely did mess up."

"Does Loreen already have some guy?" Louis couldn't imagine that a girl like Loreen would ever have gone with anyone like Maurice.

Maurice turned to look at Louis. "Why come you be askin' so much about this here Loreen? You gotta an interest or somethin' in Loreen?"

Louis wasn't sure whether or not he should admit to Maurice how he felt. "She's kinda pretty."

"Loreen don't want no dudes hangin' around her 'cause she don't want no babies. All that Loreen likes is school and workin'. She ain't gunna be gettin' herself worked up about you, I can be tellin' you that."

"That's fine with me. I like girls like that. I never did like the ones that hang out all the time. I kind of thought..." Louis stopped talking. He didn't know why, but he didn't want Maurice to know that he preferred girls who were interested in getting an education. It would be nice to have a girlfriend who would understand his own plans to do something with his life. "Do you think Loreen would like someone like me?"

"How I be knowin' what that girl like? I sure know'd she

ain't interested in no dude like me." Maurice watched Louis' face. It was as if he could see that face next to Loreen's. They would be talking and laughing together. They would share something that Maurice knew he could never share with Loreen. As much as Maurice disliked the boy who sat across from him, he thought he would be the sort of person who would be nice to Loreen.

It suddenly occurred to Maurice that Loreen deserved someone nice. In the thoughts that marched through Maurice's head, he believed that if somehow he could be a part of putting Louis into Loreen's life, it would make up for what he had done to Marvin.

"I know where Loreen lives, and I know where she be workin' and I know where she go. I knows all kinds of things about Loreen."

The information that Maurice offered surprised Louis. He was waiting for Maurice to try bribing him in exchange for finding out more about Loreen. "I just said she was a pretty girl. I didn't say I was interested."

Maurice leaned forward on his arms so that he was very close to Louis. Though Maurice did not have many of the abilities he needed to survive in school, he did understand people. He could read their faces. "Loreen now she be okay. Them crazy dudes be botherin' her and all up in her face all the time. She don't like none of that. Loreen she be needin' a nice dude. Maybe she be needin' a dude like you, Louis. What do you say?"

The suspicion Louis had of Maurice's intentions faded away. He wasn't sure why Maurice's behavior had suddenly changed, but for some reason he believed Maurice wanted him to meet Loreen. "Do you like Loreen yourself? I don't want to be moving in on you or anything like that."

"Sure I be likin' Loreen."

"Then what's your point, man?" Why are you telling me all this stuff about her?"

Maurice thought about all that Loreen was missing in life. How her days were filled with studying and going to work. When she came home from school and work there was Marvin to look after. "Loreen ain't nothin' but good. I be thinkin' that maybe Loreen needs somethin' good to happen to her. Like she don't need to be takin' care of Marvin all the time 'cause Trash Face be runnin' them streets. There ain't no decent dudes where Loreen be livin'. You is smart. You gunna be somethin'. You ain't nothin' like me, and Loreen ain't got no use for me."

"I'll think about it."

"You take that girl out, you better do right by her or I be comin' after you. I fix you good, you hear. You ever do anythin' to hurt Loreen and I fix you. You hear me, man. You better be listenin' real good." Maurice held tightly to Louis' wrist.

Louis yanked his hand free. "Don't be threatening me, man." Some of the earlier feelings of distrust for Maurice came back.

"I ain't threatenin'. I be promisin'. I ain't never gunna let nothin' happen to Loreen."

"If you don't want me to ask Loreen out, then why are you telling me all this stuff about her?"

117

"I ain't be for sure sayin' nothing' about not takin' her out." Maurice was almost whispering. "You listen up. You talk to her real nice. Don't be tryin' to act like no cool dude. You be real polite. You talk to her real nice. I know'd what kinda dude Loreen be likin'. You act like you gots some home training, and Loreen let you be coming around. You know what I mean?"

"Yeah. I got the picture."

"None of that there jive talk and struttin' around. Runnin' your mouth about what a big man you be. Loreen she don't care nothin' about that stuff. You be nice to little Marvin. That be Loreen's nephew. Loreen surely do love little Tough Stuff."

The bell sounded. "Well, we sure got a lot of studying done."

"I ain't interested in no studyin' anyhow."

Louis watched Maurice pick up his books. He felt sorry for the huge boy who was failing everything. "I'd help you if you'd let me."

"I ain't gunna be around here much longer. I hate this place." Maurice walked out the door and left the building.

Louis hurried down the hall to his English class. During most of the class he kept his eyes on Loreen. From where he sat he could see only the side of her face. Louis liked the way her nose turned up and the way she pulled her hair back and clipped it with a large red clamp.

Mrs. Young was talking about the novel the class had been reading. "Let's just try to cover some of your feelings about *The Tale of Two Cities*. We don't have to get into the details

118

at this time. Right now I'd simply like to get some of your reactions to the story. Loreen, if you had to sum up the novel in a few words, what would you say it was all about?"

Louis welcomed the chance to have a reason to stare at her while she answered the teacher's question.

"It be about these two men who look alike. One man he's a really good man. The other character, well, he..." Loreen had to stop and think. "Well, it's like he wasn't all that good. In the end, though, this man that wasn't so good, he ended up giving up his life when he took the place of the good man who was going to get his head chopped off."

"If you could only use a few words to describe what took place at the end of the novel, what words would you use, Lamont?"

Lamont scraped the toe of his shoe along the floor. "I guess I'd say sacrifice. He was willing to give up his life so that another person could live. He knew this lady loved the other man. He was going to give up his life because he loved this lady and he thought she would be happier with the man they was going to kill."

Louis thought back on what he had read, trying to recall those last few lines of the book. Louis raised his hand.

"Yes, Louis. What would you like to add?"

"Didn't Dickens write something about...? Anyhow, when he was writing about this man giving up his life, didn't he say something like *it's a far, far better thing I do now than I have ever done before?*"

"Yes, Louis. That's about what Dickens said. Does that have some special meaning to you?"

"I sort of figured he meant that his life had been useless and meaningless, and that he didn't mind sacrificing his life because it made him feel better about himself than he had ever felt before. Kinda like in the end, he made up for all the rotten things he had done in his life. The love he had for the lady was so great, he was willing to sacrifice his life for that love."

"Do you mean," the teacher asked, "that one's final act can wipe out a life of mistakes?"

"Sort of," Louis answered. Louis' thoughts drifted toward Maurice. Louis was sure that Maurice must believe his own life was rather useless and meaningless. Then Louis glanced over at Loreen. He decided that he would find some reason for talking to her after class.

CHAPTER TWELVE

The call that Jean had been expecting finally came. Flo pleaded with her to come and talk with Maurice. "I don't know what else to do, Jean. He goes to school less and less. I know he's lying to me. He leaves here in the morning and tells me he's going to school. The school has called me, though, and he's not there. I can't keep taking off work to be hunting him down. It's just a matter of time before he gets himself in some sort of trouble."

"You know I'll help, Flo. Will he be home tonight?"

"It's not likely. The only way I could keep him home is to nail him down."

"What about tomorrow night? You could tell him that I'm coming."

"I can't think of anything that would drive him out of the house faster. I think you're the last person he'd probably want to face. When he first came home from Morton Hills he kept telling me he was going to make you proud of him. He's fallen far short of that."

"Can't Loreen help? I know he thought the world of her. Won't he listen to her?"

"They've had a falling out."

"Really. That surprises me. She was so determined to help him and to be his friend."

Flo couldn't bring herself to tell Jean what she suspected had happened between Loreen and Maurice. "He hasn't seen her in months."

"I'll be by then. An unexpected call. I'll chance it that he'll be there. Better yet, suppose I take a day off and go to school. Am I likely to catch him there at all?"

"Maybe on a Monday or Tuesday. As the week wears on, he gets more notions about not going."

On the day following Flo's phone call Jean went to Kennedy High School. The principal welcomed the help of Maurice's former teacher. "He really doesn't belong here," Mr. Patterson said. "The work is just beyond him. We've assigned him a tutor, but the boy says that Maurice won't even open the book anymore."

"From what I know of Maurice, Mr. Patterson, I'd say if he did open the book, he wouldn't be able to read it. Is there anyway you could help me get him in one of the alternative high schools? Maybe one of the trade schools even."

"Some of those schools aren't what they used to be. I mean it takes a lot more work to get through them. The students still come up against regular classes. There's no getting around it, Mrs. Bestie, there are going to be a given number of regular classroom courses that Maurice is going to have to take no matter what type of school he attends."

"You'd have to agree, though, that his chances might be better in an alternative school."

"Somewhat. Certainly somewhat better."

"Then will you help me? This is what I was trying to get through before Maurice left Morton Hills. I thought it was a bad placement to send him to a regular high school."

"I'm not making any promises. I will see what I can do. Now does Maurice know you were coming today?"

"He doesn't have a clue that I'm here."

Mr. Patterson pulled Maurice's folder from a file cabinet.

"He's with his tutor in a study hall on the second floor. That might be as good a place as any for you to talk with him. The only other choice is to let you use the outer office. I doubt that Maurice would be comfortable there. He'd probably feel as if he were in some sort of trouble, which he is most of the time anyhow."

Jean followed Mr. Patterson up to the second floor. He pointed to a door at the end of the hall. "You'll find him in there."

Jean pulled the door open. Maurice was laying on the floor sleeping and the other boy was reading a book. She felt a pain in her stomach as she recalled how many days Maurice had chosen to sleep on the floor rather than to try to learn. "What's the matter, Maurice? You didn't get caught up on all your sleep at Morton Hills?"

Maurice jumped up. "PB! What you be doin' here?" Maurice looked from her to Louis.

The other boy started piling his books together.

"This here is Louis. He be my tutor."

"Is he tutoring you on how to sleep?"

The color rushed to Louis' face. "Big Mo is not too much into learning." Louis tried to explain.

"Tell me about it." Jean was not judging the boy. "Would you mind excusing us so that I can talk to Maurice?"

"No, ma'am." Louis picked up his books and bolted out the door. He was more than relieved to be out of the room.

Maurice wouldn't look at Jean. He sat down in his chair and thumped his pen on the table. "You fed up with me I suppose."

"The word on you isn't all that great. Your Auntie Flo says that you're not going to school."

"Here I be." Maurice waved his arm around the room. "This be school as far as I know."

"Now come on, Maurice. You know darn well what I'm talking about. You're cutting about half of your classes when you're here. I took a look at your attendance record when I was in Mr. Patterson's office. In three months you've missed about twenty-three days of school. So what am I supposed to believe?"

Maurice zig-zagged his pen across his book.

"Maurice, don't write on the book. For gosh sakes books cost money. Why would you want to ruin the book?" Jean's voice showed that she was annoyed.

Maurice threw the book across the room. "Stupid books. Them all stupid books."

"Are you back to throwing books, Maurice?" Jean was sorry that she had become angry with him. She'd forgotten how difficult learning was for him. "Get the book, Maurice. Let's see what's in it. Okay?" She covered his hand with her own. "Let's just take a look at what it is that's making you so angry."

Maurice slid out of his chair and picked up the book. He slammed it down on the table. "Ain't nothin' in there that I be wantin' to know."

Jean flipped through the pages. "Do you know what chapter you're on?"

Maurice turned the book around and pushed at the pages. "There. All about that government junk. Who be carin' what

124

be happenin' two hundred years ago?"

He had turned the pages to the settling of the West. "It's about how your country was settled by pioneers. Do you know what a pioneer is?"

"Them's those peoples ridin' in covered wagons."

"Yes," Jean answered. "They traveled hundreds of miles through the wilderness. It's not like they had restaurants to stop at or motels. They had it pretty rough. Can you even imagine what it must have been like to leave everything you knew behind and go off to some strange place? The women had to leave all the things they cared about. It was like they had to make decisions about what they could bring with them because the wagons would only hold so much. They couldn't bring their dishes or their pianos or things that mattered to them. They could just take what they absolutely had to have."

"PB, I don't be carin' nothin' about them women and their pianos."

"Suppose you had to leave for some place right now, Maurice, and you could only take three of the things with you that you valued most. What would take?"

"I ain't goin' nowheres."

"Imagine that you are. What would you take?"

"My radio."

"You can't take that. It's too heavy."

"I ain't gunna go nowhere without my blaster."

"But you have to go, and you can't take that. Think of something else that you'd want to take."

"All my clothes so's I could be lookin' cool."

"You can't take all your clothes. You can only take two

125

changes of clothing."

"Hey, PB, I ain't gunna go on no trip if I can't take my blaster and my duds. Them's important to me."

"What the women had to leave behind was important to them. You see, Maurice, you and the women who lived in the eighteen hundreds had something in common after all."

"Why they have to be leavin' all their stuff behind? I don't even know why they wantin' to be goin' in the first place."

"Freedom. Land. A chance to start over. If you could start all over again, would you be willing to leave your radio and clothes behind?"

"You mean like I sorta be gettin' a second chance?"

"Yes. You could go some place and you wouldn't have to work for anyone but yourself. You could have your own piece of land. You and your family could work that land, and it would be your land. Going West was for those people like..." Jean smiled. "Like going to the other side of the sun. They had no idea what was out there waiting for them, but going meant there was a new way of life waiting for them."

"This here book don't say nothing about all that stuff."

"How would you know? You haven't even read the book."

"Lookee here." Maurice shoved the book in front of her. "See them words. You know'd I don't be knowin' them words."

"I know, Maurice. I know." Her eyes glanced down the page of the book. She was more than aware it was not a book that he could read. "I've talked to Mr. Patterson. He's going to try to get you in one of the alternative high schools, which

126

is what I wanted in the first place."

"Oh, no." Maurice waved his hands in front of her. "I ain't be goin' to none of them special ed schools for the retards. You ain't no way sendin' me to one of them there schools."

"Maurice, you can't make it here. You know that now. You have to know that. Wouldn't you rather go to a school where you can succeed than to come here day after day and fail?"

"I ain't failin' nothin'."

"You are. You're failing everything. There is not one class that you're going to pass." Jean twisted her fingers together. She had to fight the urge to grab his shoulders and shake him. Instead she changed the subject. "Auntie Flo says that you and Loreen had a falling out. What happened, Maurice?"

"That be my business."

"Loreen was your friend. She wanted to help you. I remember all those nice letters you wrote her and that she wrote you. Something pretty awful must have happened."

Maurice stood up and flung the chair across the room. "I don't want no one buttin' into my business. You come up here like you some important teacher buttin' into my business. I ain't nothin' to you. You ain't nothin' to me."

"You're fighting me, Maurice." Jean stood up and walked to the window where he stood. "Your skull isn't that thick. Can't you get it through your head that I'm trying to help? Your aunt's trying to help. Loreen tried to help. What has to happen to you before you realize that before any of us can help you, you have to try to help yourself?"

Maurice's voice choked up. "I ain't worth helpin'. I just mess up. Don't you get it, PB, I ain't smart. I ain't never gunna be able to make it in school.

"And don't you get it either, Maurice? You had some tough breaks to start with. But you can't go on angry about the past. It's not too late. You're only seventeen. You can get some training if you'll go to a school that offers training. Why is it so important that you keep trying to succeed in a school where you know you're going to fail?"

"I so sick of failin', PB." Maurice pounded his fist on the wall. "I just so sick of bein' a nobody. A dumb nobody. Louis he try to help me. I don't get nothin' what he talkin' about. He try to show me how to read and make them notes in my book." Maurice's eyes filled with tears. "Ain't no way I can do it."

PB put her arms around him. "Maurice, I know that when you can do the work, you'll do it. I saw that at Morton Hills. There's nothing so horrible about admitting you can't do the work here. There's no shame in it. No one will think less of you. Make a good decision, Maurice. Please, for the sake of all us who care about you, will you make a good decision?"

Maurice leaned his head against the window pane and rocked back and forth. "You really think I can be makin' it at that other school?"

"It won't be easy, but it will be easier than here."

"Louis ain't gunna be helpin' me no more if I be goin' to that other school. Louis be my only friend here."

"Was that the boy who was here?"

"Yeah. He be okay. He tells me all about Loreen and Marvin. Loreen be his girl now."

Jean felt there were many things about the story that she didn't understand, but she was afraid to ask too many questions for fear of upsetting him. "He seems like a nice boy."

"I betcha ain't no one ever be sayin' Maurice is a nice boy. Ain't that funny?" Maurice smiled. "Louis and Loreen they be okay."

"I think you're a nice boy. Once you settled down, I thought you were a really nice boy."

"But I always need settlin' down. Ain't nobody gotta settle Louis down. He come already settled." Maurice traced his finger back and forth along the edge of the window pane. "I gotta be thinkin' more about this here other school. I ain't made my mind up yet no way. Okay."

"Okay. Will you call me? Will you let me know what you want to do? Or let Mr. Patterson know. He wants to help, too."

"Oh, Lordy. Everybody just wantin' to be helping poor old Maurice."

"Make sure that you're one of those who wants to help poor old Maurice, will you?" Jean patted him on the shoulder before she left. As she started down the hall she saw Louis leaning against the wall. She started to speak to him, but she only smiled and went past him. Then she turned around and went back to where the boy stood.

"Maurice used to be one of my students."

"Yes, ma'am."

"He says that you know Loreen."

"Yes, ma'am."

"Do you think it's possible for you to ask Loreen if she'd mind talking with me?"

"About Maurice?"

"Yes. I think Loreen could help. As a matter of fact, I think *you* could help. Do you think the two of you would be willing to help me try to talk Maurice into going to an alternative school?"

Louis looked from one end of the hall to the other. He knew what Maurice had done to Marvin and how Loreen hated him for placing the baby's life in danger. "I don't know, ma'am. Loreen is still pretty upset with Maurice. All I got to do is say his name and she goes off."

"Would you ask her? Would you just ask for me, please?"

"Yes, ma'am."

"Here's my phone number. Maybe you or Loreen could call me? Louis....Is that right?"

"Yes, ma'am. Louis Halstead."

"Louis, it's like the last chance for Maurice. Somehow we've all got to show him we care. He says that you tried to help him and that you were his friend."

"Maurice said that about me!" Louis looked surprised. "He never said anything about my being his friend."

"That's what he told me."

Louis wondered if she were lying in the hopes that he would help her if he thought Maurice had called him his friend. "Maurice can't do the work. I know. I tried to help him and he just doesn't get it. It's like he tried a few times, but he never knows what I'm talking about."

"I understand. It's going to take a teacher with some special training to help Maurice. I'm sure you did a good job, Louis, but the job was bigger than one that you could handle. You will ask Loreen, won't you?"

"Yes, ma'am. I'll see her tonight and I'll ask her."

"Thank you."

Loreen's answer was as Louis had expected. She clearly refused to have anything to do with Maurice. Louis tried to reason with her. "Maybe we could just talk to that teacher. You don't have to see Maurice. Maybe just see what the teacher wants us to do."

"How come you always be sidin' with Maurice against me?" Loreen demanded to know. "I done told you what a terrible thing he did. Ain't that reason enough to stay away from him?"

"I feel sorry for him."

"Why you be feelin' sorry for that no good? He done almost killed little Marvin. Suppose Marvin died. Then who you be feelin' sorry for?"

"Come on, Loreen. Make some sense, why don't you? There probably isn't anyone sorrier for what happened than Big Mo. Loreen, that dude doesn't have anyone. He does his best to stay away from the dealers and the punks. Some of the kids are scared to death of him and they stay away from him. The ones who do okay in school don't even know he's alive or they're laughing at him because he can't get anything right in class. He's flunking everything at school and the teachers are on his case most of the time. You don't talk to him. His aunt's about to give up on him. Big Mo doesn't have a thing going for him."

"How come you got to be such a big fan of Maurice's? You used to be tellin' me you didn't even like him."

Louis dropped his head and stared down at the floor. "I guess I really don't know. There's just something so sad about him. Like the rest of the world's moving and he's not going any place."

"He ain't goin' no place because he don't try."

"I've seen how he tried to learn. He just doesn't have it. He really did try, but he just gave up. Look at what he came out of, Loreen. That mama of his is bad news. He doesn't even know who his father is. He's got a rough way to go."

"You and me we ain't exactly on easy street. Look at you, Louis. Your mama works so hard like my mama. Your daddy only come around now and then. Yet you don't run them streets and act the fool the way that clown be doin'."

Louis wasn't sure how to handle the argument with Loreen. In the two months they had been going together they had never argued before. It bothered him that he was seeing a side of Loreen that he didn't know existed. Ever since he had first asked her out, Loreen had been everything that he had hoped she'd be. No matter what he wanted to talk about, he found that Loreen would listen. They both talked about their hopes and dreams of finishing school and one day getting good jobs. He thought she might laugh when he told her about his plans for trying to find some type of scholarship that would make it possible for him to go to college. Instead of laughing, Loreen praised him for wanting such a dream.

He'd seen nothing but kindness and gentleness from her since the first day that he'd walked her home. Arguing with her now over Maurice upset him. Louis wanted her to be able to see that somehow they owed Maurice their help.

"I think, Louis, where's we differ is that Maurice been hangin' around in my life a lot longer than you be knowin' him. He's done worn me out the same as he's done to his Auntie Flo. Here you just come along. He ain't worn you down yet."

"I guess I'm glad it's not me. Without a few breaks, I could be Maurice. My mama has loved me from the day I was born. No matter what, I knew my mama loved me. I always did okay in school. I keep thinking what my life would be like if I had a mama like Maurice and if I couldn't read or do my homework." Louis kept poking his fingers along the edge of the sofa.

"Okay." Loreen agreed as much as she was capable of agreeing. "I don't even be knowin' what you want me to be doing, but I gunna help. One more time. Only one more time and that's it."

Louis put his arm around Loreen and squeezed her shoulder. "I think that old teacher of his just wants us to be his friends. She's going to try to get him in the alternative high school."

"Hm. Hm. I know'd for a fact that Maurice ain't gunna go to no such school. He done told me that a long time ago."

"Maybe he'll go now. He's been to Kennedy High and he

133

knows he can't do it. If you and I stand by him, and sort of help him with his school work and let him know we want him to make it, well...well, maybe he'll make it."

Loreen reached over and kissed Louis. "You's a good man, Louis. Real good. I sorta feel ashamed of how...Like I be ashamed of not wantin' to help Maurice. I suppose that's why I love you 'cause you is just good. Good all the way through. You ain't no phony like them other boys. Just good."

Louis cradled Loreen in his arms. "You know, Loreen, all the time I was growing up I'd look around me and I just knew I didn't want to be like some of them that I'd see. My mama taught me that. It never seemed to matter to her how down we got ourselves, she always had time to help people. She was always telling me that good people help everyone and you shouldn't be asking too many questions as to how they got into the mess. You should try to help them out of the mess. Do you believe that?"

"I don't be knowin' for sure. I don't be havin' much patience with the bad ones. Like that sister of mine. I look and I look and I can't see no good in that girl."

"Mama sees good in about everyone she's ever met. My granddaddy was a preacher. I expect she learned a lot from him before he died. He was an educated man. From the time I was really little she was always correcting me, saying, 'Your granddaddy would turn over in his grave if he heard you talk that way.' She says I look like my granddaddy."

"How come your mama didn't stay with that daddy of yours?"

Louis laughed. "She says they married too young. They just decided to go their separate ways. He's a good man, though. We miss each other. My mama says I should be careful and not be blinded by love."

"You been blinded by love?" Loreen grinned and took his hand. "Love done knocked your eyes out or what?"

"I've just always thought you were the prettiest girl at school."

Loreen blushed. "The prettiest you say! Why, boy, there's plenty more prettier than me." Loreen looked at him and hoped that he'd deny what she said.

"Maybe one or two." He leaned his cheek against hers.

"Then be gettin' out of my face." She teased him. "Hey, I gots to be gettin' this place cleaned up before I go to work." Loreen stood up and looked around the room. "Oh, Lordy, Louis, I surely do hope that some day I be havin' better than this. I surely want me a nice place with pretty things."

"You'll get it Loreen. I'll see to that."

"You better be movin' on why I finish my cleanin'."

"Will you call Mrs. Bestie?"

"I said so didn't I?" Loreen smiled. "One more time I gunna help that Maurice. Just one more time." She poured cleanser into the sink and scrubbed at the spots. "I'd help that boy forever if I could get these nasty spots outta my sink. I surely do be hatin' dirt, Louis. I just hate dirt."

CHAPTER THIRTEEN

Maurice kept trying to tell himself that he hated the new school, but he had difficulty continuing to believe the lie. The books that some of his teachers gave him were like the ones that he used at Morton Hills. He found that he could do the assignments and that now and then he even knew the answers when teachers called on him in class.

Flo found it difficult to believe that Maurice still kept going to school everyday. She even called the school to see if Maurice had lied to her. Yes, the principal told her, Maurice was in school every day, and he was on time. No, the principal added, Maurice was not causing any trouble. For the first time in years Flo began to feel there was hope for Maurice. Many of the good feelings she had about him came from the fact that Louis had become his friend and Loreen had appeared to have forgiven Maurice.

In the evenings Flo would listen to the three of them laughing and talking in her kitchen. Over the years there had been very few of Maurice's friends whom Flo welcomed into her home. They had a look about them that made her afraid. It seemed as if they had not come to visit, but rather to look over what she owned so that they could return and steal her belongings. From the first time she met Louis, Flo liked him. The last thing she wanted Maurice to know was that she thought Louis was the nicest young man Maurice had ever brought to her home. Flo smiled to herself and wondered why young people seemed to turn against anyone whom the adults found nice.

Loreen sat rocking Marvin as Louis explained to Maurice

how to move decimal points for his math assignment. "See, Maurice, if you want to change a percent into a decimal, you move the decimal this way." Louis drew arrows to show the direction the decimal should be moved.

"I ain't never gunna get this here decimal business." Maurice bent over and watched what Louis was doing.

Loreen smacked her lips and warned Maurice to pay attention. "Just listen to yourself, boy. You always saying what you ain't never gunna be able to do. Just do like Louis be telling you. Think some good about yourself."

"She's right," Louis agreed. "If you start out thinking you won't be able to do it, chances are you won't be able to. Hey, man," Louis tapped his finger on Maurice's forehead, "you got to use your brain and think positive. Okay."

Maurice grinned at him. "You know about everythin', don't you Lou-EE?"

"Hey, boy." Loreen frowned. "Don't be callin' him no *Lou-EE*. I hate that!"

Louis jumped up and ran over to where Loreen sat holding Marvin. "I'm Lou-EE. I'm Lou-EE." He teased.

"Get your face outta my face, boy. You be acting the fool like that there Maurice." She laughed at the two of them.

"Come here, man." Maurice called out. "This here problem be different. Ain't no way to be learnin' this here stuff 'cause about the time I figure one out, this here book changes things." He turned the book around so that Louis could see it. "Lookee. Them's not the same as I be doin'. Now they got some percents and they be tellin' me to make decimals. Just all crazy stuff."

137

"You just reverse what you've been doing. You move the decimal point this way." Louis showed Maurice what to do. "Now get busy. I'm going to set the timer. You have twenty minutes to finish."

Even though Maurice hated doing his homework, he felt a sense of comfort listening to Loreen talking to Marvin and knowing that his Auntie Flo was in the living room reading the paper. The smell of stew cooking was coming from the stove behind him. Next to him sat the only boy whom Maurice ever believed had been a true friend. Maurice didn't know how to tell any of them that they all mattered to him. The words that expressed what these people meant to him finally came tumbling out when Jean took Maurice to lunch.

The restaurant was not like any that Maurice had ever been in. The tables were covered with white cloths and there seemed to be far more silverware than he thought anyone would ever use for one meal. "I ain't never eat in no place like this place." Maurice looked around at the waitresses who wore long black skirts and who were serving people who looked like people Maurice had seen in movies.

"I brought you here to celebrate."

"What we be celebratin'?"

"You passed. You passed every class. I think that's cause for celebrating. Now what are you going to order?" She watched him reading the menu, thinking back how he had once struggled with the simplest of words and now he was reading from a menu.

"What's this here stuff?" Maurice pointed to the menu. "Scalp...Hm. No. That can't be right. Ain't no restaurant got scalps." He broke out laughing. "What it be, PB?"

"Scalloped potatoes. Those are sliced potatoes that are cooked in milk. They usually have cheese mixed in with them. They're quite good."

"I'm gunna get me some of that roast beef and mashed potatoes. I don't be wantin' none of them...what you be callin' them kind of potatoes?"

"Scalloped. And you know what? I think I'll get them. Then I can give you a taste and you can decide for yourself if you like them. Maybe next time when you eat out you can order them. It's nice to have new experiences." Jean shook out her napkin and put it in her lap.

Maurice watched what she did. "That napkin go here in my lap?"

"If you want it there."

Maurice looked around at the other customers. "They all be havin' their napkins in their laps. I better be puttin' mine there." He waved his napkin as he had seen Jean do. Then he placed it in his lap. "This place be okay." He glanced around. "This be just okay."

"Well, Maurice, are you proud of yourself?"

"You be talkin' about that school?"

"I sure am. You did just great." Jean smiled at him and handed him the salad dressing. "You want some of this on your lettuce?"

Maurice took the bottle from her and eyed it. "Vin-ah-vin-ah-."

"Vinegar."

"Yeah." Maurice shook the dressing onto his own salad.

139

"I gunna be takin' cookin' this next semester. All them boys at the school gotta be takin' cookin'." Maurice laughed out loud. "We be hootin' and hollerin' about that cookin'. Ain't nobody pay us no mind. Sometimes I be helpin' Auntie Flo cook. Don't be botherin' me none. I take to that cookin'."

"You seem to have taken to everything. Heard you got a "B" in math." Jean sprinkled pepper on her salad.

"I sure did. You can be puttin' pepper on that lettuce?"

"If you like pepper on your lettuce, put it on."

"Louis helped me. I be gettin' that "B" because Louis be helpin' me." Maurice shoved a forkful of the salad in his mouth. "I ain't never had no friend like Louis. All them other dudes they be tryin' to get over on me or they be tryin' to mess with my mind. All crazy stuff is all they be carin' about. Now Louis he be makin' some sense." Maurice set his fork down and looked over at Jean. "You know I don't be knowin' how to say what's goin' on in my head, but it's like my insides is feelin' all good."

"Because of Louis?"

"Aw, it be Louis and Loreen. You and Auntie Flo. It's like there ain't all this pain and mad stuff in me no more. I gets to thinkin' about Louis comin' over to Auntie Flo's. Then Loreen she be bringin' Marvin with her. We all be just sittin' around talkin' and blowin' about school and what we gunna be doin.' I start lookin' around and listenin' to them all talkin' and such." Maurice opened up his hands and held them up as if he were struggling for the words to say what he was thinking and feeling.

"You know a few years back people used to say they felt warm and fuzzy." Jean laughed. "They were talking about this really neat feeling going on inside them."

"I ain't be feelin' no warm and fuzzy anythin'."

Now it was Jean who struggled for words. "It's like you're outside and you are really cold. Your toes are positively numb. Then you walk into your house. The house is cozy and warm. There's this pair of slippers that have been near the oven. The slippers are all fuzzy. Then you take those cold, cold feet and you slip them into those warm and fuzzy slippers." Jean closed her eyes and imagined what it would be like. "It feels great. All warm and fuzzy like they used to say."

"Yeah." A smile spread across Maurice's face. "Yeah. Real warm and fuzzy."

"You ought to tell your Auntie and your friends how you feel."

"They don't wanna be hearin' no warm and fuzzy stories about my insides."

"You'd be surprised what friends want to hear, Maurice. You just try telling them that they are important to you. You'll probably find out that you're important to them, also."

She watched him fold up slices of meat and dip them in his potatoes and gravy. His brow was folded into a frown. "Is there something the matter, Maurice?"

"Well, I be thinkin'. My Auntie Flo and Louis and Loreen, now they be givin' and givin'. Don't seem like I got much to be givin' back. I just be takin' all the time."

141

"You shouldn't overlook the fact that there is great pleasure in giving. They wouldn't be helping you and caring about you if they weren't getting something out of it."

"And what they be gettin' out of it?"

"Your love and friendship."

"That ain't nothin'. That love and friendship ain't like really givin' somethin'."

"You, young man, are dead wrong."

Maurice took his roll, broke it into pieces, and dropped them into the remaining gravy. "I gotta be workin' on what I can be doin' to be givin' more than I be takin'."

"You know one of these days, Maurice, I might be able to pound it into your head what life is really all about."

"You just stay on your J.O.B, Teach, and you just might be makin' it."

CHAPTER FOURTEEN

Maurice was running down the hall to reach class before the bell sounded. Suddenly he remembered that he had left his homework in the small annex building located next to the main building. *Darn.* Maurice stopped dead. He turned around and ran out the door toward the annex. He had made the decision that he would rather be late for class than to show up without his homework. He entered the smaller building and knocked on the door of the classroom that he had just left.

"Here you go, Maurice." His teacher handed him his notebook with the needed homework. "I saw you heading this way."

"You be givin' me a pass so as I can be gettin' back in class?"

She handed him the white slip of paper and smiled. "I had it all ready for you. And it's not *you be givin' me*. It's, 'Will you give me a pass?' Your English is horrible, Maurice."

"Yes, ma'am." Maurice ran for the door. He was racing down the sidewalk when he heard his name called. Maurice stopped and looked around. He didn't see anyone. Then he heard his name again.

"Over here, Big Mo." Hoagy stepped out from behind a building that sat away from the sidewalk. "I been looking for you Big Guy. I got some action going down. I figured I could cut you in. Ain't too many out there you can trust anymore. Interested?"

Maurice shook his head. "I ain't messin' with no drugs, Hoagy." Maurice noticed the bright blue jacket Hoagy had on. "Got yourself some kind of new threads there, Hoagy?"

143

"Yeah, Big Mo. Me and my pals is sporting these now. It sort of makes it clear where we stand if you know what I mean."

"I be hearin' you and them Falcons gunnin' for each other. Them's a bad bunch of dudes."

"Ain't nothing we can't handle. We're fixing to clear those boys out. They don't know it yet. We got time. Plenty of time." Hoagy saw how Maurice kept looking at the shiny jacket. "What do you think of the torch?" Hoagy turned around. On the back of the jacket was a red and orange emblem. "Something else, huh?"

Maurice nodded. "I gotta be gettin' to class."

"Last chance, Big Mo. This is a big one. Maybe two days work. Some deliveries around town. About ten or fifteen. We're talking some big bucks here. None of this small change stuff anymore. Me and the Torches are uptown now. I'll throw in a jacket. What do you say, Big Mo? Can I count you in?"

Maurice stood there looking at the jacket. "How much you talkin' about now that we ain't talkin' small change?"

"In the hundreds. Depends on how many drops you make. You come by and see me tomorrow morning. We'll settle up."

"I gotta be in school tomorrow."

"Hey, man," Hoagy laughed. "You some kind of kid or something? I'm not laying out green stuff for dropping white stuff if I'm working with a kid."

His words made Maurice angry. "I ain't no kid."

"Then drop on by in the morning. See you."

The sleep that Maurice tried to find that night never came. He tossed and turned until finally the rays of sun passed through his bedroom window. As he put on his clothes he kept an eye on his books that he had put on the dresser the night before. Inside his notebook was the first book report that he had ever written. Louis had gone over the report and made all the necessary corrections. Then Maurice carefully copied the report again. Maurice wanted to hand in the report and listen to the good things his teacher would say about him.

It was nearly quarter to eight when Maurice left the house. He kissed Flo goodbye, carefully avoiding her eyes because he was sure his face would give him away as to what he had decided to do. Maurice walked up to the corner as if he were waiting for his bus. Just before the bus pulled to the curb, Maurice darted into the grocery store and bought some gum. After the bus pulled away from the stop, Maurice ran out the door and headed for the other bus stop at the far end of the block.

In less than thirty minutes Maurice stepped off the bus at the corner of Taylor and Benton. He took a quick look around. Then he ran toward Hoagy's. The same young men whom Maurice had always seen with Hoagy were stretched out on the couch or laying on the floor listening to music. They offered Maurice a drag off the reefers they puffed on. Maurice shook his head.

"Smart move, Big Mo." Hoagy stepped out from the kitchen. "I tell my boys they'd be better off leaving it all alone. Stay clean." Hoagy tapped his temple. "Stay clean

and don't hurt that brain of yours." He motioned for Maurice
to follow him. "Over there. That's the drops. That little old
dude would come in handy about now."

Maurice was quick to answer. "Ain't gunna be no more
babies in on this. Hear, man?"

"Loud and clear." Hoagy stacked up the plastic bags.
"This is big money, so you take it easy and careful. No foul
ups. Got it?"

"I witcha, man." Maurice eyed the jackets the others were
wearing. "You be promisin' me one of them jackets. You
comin' across or not?"

Hoagy opened a closet in the kitchen, reached in and
grabbed a jacket. "Ain't no problem, man. Ain't no problem
at all. Glad to have you joining us."

Maurice slipped on the jacket. "You want me comin' back
here or what?"

"You got it. Don't be dragging your tail either. I want all
this out on the streets before six tonight. Can you handle it?"

"Like you be sayin', Hoagy, ain't no problem." Maurice
lifted up one leg of his pants and one by one strapped the
packages around his calf as Hoagy dropped the small plastic
straps on the floor. "Be back by about six. Now I be outta
here."

With each stop, Maurice replaced the clear plastic bag with
the cash that was turned over to him. It was close to noon
when Maurice stopped for a hamburger. He walked along
eating and looking in the windows at the things he planned to
buy Louis and Loreen. Suddenly he felt a pair of hands push
him.

"Hey, what you got on your mind, you..." Maurice turned and saw the two flaming red jackets. He looked down at the knife pressing against his stomach. One of the young men nodded toward the alley. The other one spun Maurice around and shoved him toward the dumpsters in the alley.

Neither of the men said a word as they ran their hands up and down Maurice's body. Then the one smiled as his hands touched the drugs and the money. He slipped the knife between Maurice's calf and the strap, making small nicks in Maurice's leg as he cut the bags loose. One of them bent down to pick up the money and drugs. He smiled and said, "You be sure and tell Hoagy we was asking about him and his health." As quickly as they had come, they were gone.

Maurice ran all the way to Hoagy's. Before he even sat down, Maurice was trying to explain what happened. Hoagy handed Maurice a soda. He stood silently over where Maurice sat until Maurice had finished telling him how the Red Wings had taken the drugs and the money. Hoagy only said, "Them is the breaks. You can't help bad luck."

"Hey, Hoagy, they was all over me in seconds. Lookee here." Maurice showed him the blood that ran down his leg. "Them no goods cut me up."

Hoagy walked around in front of Maurice's chair. He placed his foot under the front legs of the chair and pulled the legs out from under Maurice, knocking Maurice to the floor. "They don't come much more stupid than you."

"Whatcha talkin' about, man? Them guys be holdin' a knife on me."

"Is that a fact? Now here I thought they'd be asking you if

you minded them taking what belonged to old Hoagy." Hoagy bent down and put his face close to Maurice's. "You dumbhead, what do you think is going down out there? Ain't you been around long enough to know how it's played out there? You should have shot them."

"I don't got no gun." Maurice picked himself up off the floor. "I ain't never had no gun."

"Then you better get one 'cause you got two choices, Big Mo. You can get a gun and find our friends and take care of business, or you can come up with the three big ones that you owe me."

"Whatcha be talkin' about them big ones?"

"Three thousand bucks."

Maurice's mouth dropped at the mention of the money. "I ain't got no three thousand bucks."

"First you say you ain't got a gun to see that matters are settled. Now you're telling me you ain't got three thousand bucks. Well, man, I'm telling you, and you better be listening, you need to be coming up with one or the other or you're going to be walking around carrying your head in your hands."

Maurice's hands started perspiring. His stomach churned with cramps. "They's a gang. I ain't goin' after no gang. You be my gang. Lookee here." Maurice took hold of the front of his blue jacket. "I be in your gang. You gotta back me. Friends look after friends."

"You ain't no friend of mine." Hoagy pulled the jacket down around Maurice's shoulders and pushed him against the wall. "No dumbheads in my little group. I gave you a jacket.

148

Nothing more. Now get out of here and start figuring out how you're going to settle this. Shoot one of them or deliver me some money." Hoagy opened the door and shoved Maurice out.

That night Maurice was as restless as he had been the night before. Getting a gun would not be a problem. He knew several boys at school who had guns. Shooting someone was not something Maurice believed himself capable of doing. It made no sense to have a gun if he couldn't do what Hoagy told him he had to do. Maurice could not even think where he might get the money that Hoagy demanded. It was impossible for Maurice to even imagine how large a sum three thousand dollars was.

Long before the sun came up, Maurice sat at the kitchen table and cried. When Flo got up she only had to look at him to know that something was very wrong. "What is it, Maurice? You look like death is knocking at your door."

Maurice looked at her and thought how close she was to guessing the truth. "Ain't nothin', Auntie Flo. That old school be gettin' me down."

Flo closed her eyes and bit her lip. She knew she didn't have anymore energy left to deal with him if he were again going to drop out of school. "Now I thought things were going just fine. You passed everything. You're in that shop class learning how to fix cars. That's what you wanted. What's going wrong now?"

"Just ain't nothin'." Maurice stood up and walked to his room. He was relieved that she didn't follow him, and that she left for work without again trying to find out why he was so upset. Soon after he heard the front door close, Maurice went back into the kitchen and poured some cereal into a bowl. He started to take a bite, but the taste of food only made him feel sick. Maurice picked up the bowl and threw it on the floor. Then he went into the bathroom and vomited.

For hours Maurice sat in Flo's living room. Every thought he had as to how he could save himself disappeared with the answers he gave himself as to why the plan would not work. If he went to the police, he would be arrested himself. Hoagy had as many friends in jail as he had on the street. Maurice knew if he were locked up, his fate would be worse than if Hoagy found him on the streets. Hiding out at his mother's would only delay what Maurice knew Hoagy would do to him when he finally found him. Remaining at Flo's was out of the question. The last person in the world he wanted harmed because of what he had done was his aunt.

Exhausted from worrying, Maurice finally dozed off for nearly two hours. As he stirred awake his mind instantly thought of the problem that seemed to have no solution. Maurice stood up and paced around the room. The faces of his aunt and friends came to mind. He could see those faces and how they'd look at him if they knew what he had done and how he now had to pay for what had happened.

Rain started spattering the windows. Maurice reached over and turned on a light. Then he looked over at the china cabinet where Flo kept what she called her *treasures*. Maurice opened the doors of the glass cabinet. Carefully he examined each of the plates and silver that sat behind the glass. They were the treasure's that Flo's husband had bought her.

Flo often went to the cabinet and held some of her treasures in her hand while she told Maurice about her husband and how proud he was that he could buy her so many nice things. "He was a hard worker that man was." Flo would smile when she recalled her husband. "When we were young and first married we didn't have much. I used to tell him how one day I'd like to set a fine table covered with crystal and silver. He'd pat my hand and assure me that one day it would be just like I dreamed. And it was."

Maurice bent his head down as he leaned against the cabinet. Maurice drove away thoughts of how Flo would feel when she found out that he had taken those things that she valued most. Hoagy, though, had to be paid off.

Maurice went to his bedroom and yanked a blanket off the bed. Quickly he spread the blanket on the floor. He hurriedly removed the silverware and several of the silver plates from the cabinet. The rainbows that gleamed on the crystal figurines as the light hit the tiny figures made Maurice think they were pretty enough to be of value. He stuck two of the smallest in his pockets. Then he ran into the kitchen and took out a large trash bag and shoved the blanket and its contents into the plastic bag.

As he ran out the door, Maurice took one last look around, knowing that he would never be able to come back. He boarded the bus. His hands shook as he held tightly to the bag that he placed in the seat next to him. The headache that he had woke up with had grown so painful that Maurice felt dizzy and sick to his stomach. As the bus passed the school, he turned his head. He didn't allow himself to think about where he had been or about the good things he had been doing with his life.

The pawn shop to which Maurice was heading was four blocks from the bus stop. Maurice didn't hurry as he did not want to draw any attention to himself for fear he might be noticed by the police. For several minutes he stood in a doorway while he waited for a squad car to pull away from the curb and turn the corner at the next block. Then Maurice picked up the bag and walked to the entrance of the pawn shop.

The man behind the counter placed his hands beneath the counter and moved them along until his fingers touched the gun that he kept nearby. Always there was a doubt in his mind if those who walked through the door had entered in the hopes of getting money for the property they brought to him, or if they had come to rob him. "Morning." He eyed Maurice and kept his hands on the gun.

"Mornin'." Maurice lifted the bag up to the counter. Then he reached in his pocket and took out the crystal figurines. "My auntie she be givin' me some stuff 'cause I done good in school."

The man's expression did not change. He never smiled. "Is that so?" He fingered the figurines and watched as Maurice unrolled the blanket and showed him the silverware.

"She don't be havin' no money to give me or nothin' like that so's she done give me this stuff. How much you be givin' me?"

The man touched several pieces of the silverware. "It's

quality silver." He took one of the larger bowls over to the light and held it up. "Fine quality. I think I could give you a fair price. I need to check my books."

"Whatcha mean check your books?"

"These type of items have a market value. I can only offer what I'm likely to get back. With a profit, of course." He tried to sound somewhat more friendly. "A man's got to make a living you know." He placed the silver bowl back on top of the blanket. "I won't be but a minute." He stepped away from the counter and disappeared behind a curtain that separated the front of the store from his living quarters in the back. In a few minutes he returned with a large blue notebook. "Let me see here what we got. P. Q. R. S. Here we go. Silver." He peered over his glasses. What would you say the dimensions of this bowl are?" He held up the silver bowl.

"I don't be knowin' nothin' about no dimenceons."

The pawnbroker reached over and pulled out a tape measure and stretched it across the top of the bowl. "Eight inches. Now let me see what the book says." He drew his finger down the page. Before he reached the bottom of the page, the shop door flew open and two police officers walked in.

They both held guns on Maurice. One said, "Just nice and easy. Put your hands up and don't do anything that looks like you might be going to ruin my morning." He moved closer to Maurice. "Now if you would be so kind as to turn around and bend over that counter, we can get right to the point of finding out if some place on that thieving body of yours you got a gun."

He spun Maurice around and shoved his face down on the counter. "Spread the legs, sonny." The officer ran his hands up and down Maurice's body. "No hardware." He put his gun in his holster. "Okay, Billy, you want to run it on out what went down so I can see what we got here."

The man looked at Maurice. "He just came in here with this bag. He said his aunt gave him the stuff." Billy shook his head. "I can't think of a story that I haven't heard. One's nuttier than the last one."

The officer who identified himself as Officer O'Fallon took hold of Maurice's jacket and pulled him forward. "One of the Torches, huh. Now there's a bunch for you." O'Fallon turned and looked at his partner. "Anybody would be proud to call those boys their own. They ought to take the whole bunch out, line them up, and shoot them."

"I ain't no Torch." Maurice denied the officer's accusation. "My friend just be givin' me this here jacket."

"Yeah," O'Fallon said, "and my grandma robs banks. So where did you pick up your little bag of goodies?"

"They's mine."

"I knew it." The other officer smiled. "All we had to do was ask and we'd get the truth. Okay, kid. Get it together and run it past me where you got this stuff. I don't have time to be messing around with no punk."

Maurice looked up at the old tin ceiling. The patterns in the tin appeared to be whirling around. "I ain't got nothing to say."

"How old are?" Officer O'Fallon asked.

"Seventeen."

Officer O'Fallon looked Maurice up and down. "They must feed you well. Come on, let's haul him into juvenile."

"You be puttin' me in jail and they be killin' me."

"Who's going to kill you?"

Maurice made no move when the officer took hold of Maurice's arm. "It don't matter none."

"That's the problem with all too many of you. Nothing matters." The officer turned and said to Billy, "We'll be back for a statement."

The other officer threw the blanket over the silver. "Anything else?"

Billy held up the crystal figurines. "These went with his things."

"Not *his* things. They belong to the poor character that this here sticky fingers lifted them off of." The officer dropped the figurines into the blanket. "See you, Billy. And thanks for the tip."

Officer O'Fallon read Maurice his rights. Then he put his hand on the top of Maurice's head, eased his head downward to place him in the back of the patrol car. "You want to tell us who to call or do we have to find that out on our own?"

"Ain't nobody to call."

"There has to be someone who's in charge of your life."

"No." Maurice shook his head. "Ain't nobody in charge of me. My mama she..." Maurice fought back the tears. "She not be carin' no way what I be doin'."

"That figures."

Maurice leaned back in the seat. He stared out the window, wondering if any of those whom he saw hurrying along the streets could ever be as angry with life as he was today.

CHAPTER FIFTEEN

Flo poured Jean a cup of tea. Neither of them felt as if they could say anything to comfort one another. "That's a new kind of tea. It has cinnamon and lemon. I've never heard of mixing the two, have you?" Flo handed her the cup.

"I might have tried something like it. There's just so many different brands out now."

"It's almost more than a body can deal with shopping nowadays what with so many different brands of everything. I think we'd do better if we had fewer choices." There was something about her mentioning choices that made her cry.

Jean reached over and put an arm around Flo. "I know you must feel like you're caught in a nightmare."

"Yes." Flo wiped at her eyes. "I do."

"I'm trying to get up the courage to visit him at Juvenile Hall. Right now I don't think I can face him. Can you believe that makes me feel guilty? He's the one who stole the things and here *I feel* guilty. It's crazy. Just crazy." Jean stood up and walked back and forth across the room. Her eyes saw the empty places in the china cabinet.

Flo saw Jean staring at the shelves. "I swear, Jean." Flo raised her voice and shook her fist. "That boy knew how much those things meant to me. I'd tell him stories about my Fred and how he bought me those things. Of all the things in the house, why did he have to take something that meant so much to me?"

"Why did he take anything of yours? Or anyone's for that matter. I can just hear him saying how he didn't mean to mess

157

up and now that he's messed up, how he's not going to matter to anyone. It's like a record, Flo. Like some darn old record that he keeps playing. He gets us all feeling sorry for him, and then he turns around and messes up again."

Flo blew her nose. "You know I can't take him back anymore. I just can't."

"No one is blaming you, Flo. There's not another thing that you can do. He's in some kind of serious trouble and he won't talk about it. The police know it. You and I know it. What's the use?" Jean threw her hands up in the air. "We keep beating our heads against a wall to help him and he just keeps screwing up."

"It's the drugs."

Jean sat down again and sipped at the tea. "Do you think he's using drugs?"

Flo shook her head. "I never did see one sign of that. But somehow I know there are drugs involved. Those horrible little pills and powder can drive them all to ruin. That's all it could be."

"You're probably right. Do you have any idea what you're going to do?"

"About prosecuting?"

"Yes. I know that has to be a terrible decision for you. What have the police suggested?"

"They don't have the answers. They just have his statement and the evidence. A bag full of some of the most important things in my life." Flo walked over to the cabinet and pressed her hands against the glass. "You know how important Maurice is to me, but I can't take him back." She repeated her position again. "I can't do anymore for him."

"I take it you're not going to prosecute."

"No. I can't be the one who sends him away, but I can't take him back. That's what is just plain eating at me, Jean. Where does he go? He'll be out on those streets and into worse than this. That tramp mother of his isn't going to do anything. She probably doesn't even know where he is now. Oh, Jean, I wish with all my heart that I could take him back with me, but I can't."

"Flo, you're going to make yourself crazy if you keep this up. Maybe you ought to prosecute. At least that way he'll be convicted and sent to some..." Jean couldn't finish.

"You were going to say to some prison."

"It won't be prison. He's too young. Probably the city work house."

"He's only seventeen."

"That doesn't matter much anymore. He just has too many charges against him. I know for a fact he won't go back to Morton Hills. He's too risky for a group home. There's the possibility that maybe his case worker can get him sent to Alton."

"What's that?"

"It's like a...It's not a prison, but it's a minimum security place. Some of the eighteen and nineteen-year-olds are being sent there. I know several boys who ended up there after Morton Hills. The only problem is, it usually takes a more serious offense than what Maurice has done. He's sort of caught in the middle here. He's done too many things to get

159

himself in trouble so a group home is out, and he doesn't have enough violations for a place like Alton. That's why I think it will be the work house if you prosecute."

"That place is disgusting. One time I visited one of Fred's relatives there. Lordy. Dirty. You could hear the cursing and the yelling from the time you walked in the door. They just sit around in those cells all day with nothing to do. No, Jean. I couldn't be the one who puts Maurice there."

"Are you going to visit him?"

"Not yet. I just can't. He'll be released to his mother if I don't prosecute. That Officer O'Fallon called this morning about it. He said he didn't think I'd come through and take Maurice to court. You know he didn't even seem angry or anything. It was as if he expected me to drop the charges. He told me if I did drop the charges that he'd bring my things back by. They were holding them for evidence, you know."

"Yes. I know how it goes." Jean put the cup down. "Is there anything I can do, Flo? Anything at all?"

"You're a kind woman, Jean. What I don't understand is how you work with so many of them that are like Maurice."

"I enter the classroom everyday with hope, Flo. There are just enough of them who make it to keep me going. Not all of them end up like Maurice. There's a lot of them who pull through despite all the horrible things that have happened to them. And believe me, a lot of them don't get the breaks Maurice had, and a lot of them don't have any Auntie Flo who'll do what you did."

"We'll be in touch."

Jean hugged Flo and walked out the door.

160

In the months that followed Jean often thought about Maurice and wondered where he was and what it was he was doing. As the weeks passed by, the anger Flo felt for him began to disappear and she called Loreen to see if she knew where Maurice might be. Loreen remained less forgiving. She was still filled with anger toward Maurice. The anger was so strong that she never told Louis that Flo had called and was willing to give Maurice one more chance.

The thing that Loreen wanted most was for Maurice to be out of her life forever. That was not possible as long as Louis continued to see Maurice. They had argued for weeks when Loreen found out that Louis knew where Maurice was and that he was still determined to help him. After a while Loreen agreed that she wouldn't argue with Louis anymore, but she didn't want to hear anything more about Maurice and how he was living.

Like the others who cared about Maurice, Louis at first abandoned him. Louis was more than disgusted with Maurice and what he had done. Then as Louis thought more about Maurice's situation, Louis came to accept the fact that something must have driven Maurice to do what he did.

If for no other reason than to find out why Maurice had hurt Flo so much, Louis went in search of his friend. Louis recalled that Maurice once had told him how he hid in the basement of his mother's building. There were many nights when her men friends would start drinking and Maurice feared what they might do to him. He'd go to the basement and hide. Maurice felt safe there because there was a door behind a pile of boxes. The door led to yet another basement that led to the vacant building next to his mother's. When he'd hear footsteps, Maurice would slip behind the boxes and through the door and upstairs to one of the empty apartments in the empty building. It was in one of those empty, rat-filled rooms that Louis finally found Maurice.

Maurice heard someone call his name. He pressed himself into one of the closets and waited. At first Maurice thought that the voice belonged to Hoagy or one of Hoagy's friends. Maurice couldn't believe that Hoagy could have found him after looking so many times for him at his mother's. After months of searching, it seemed to Maurice that Hoagy had given up.

"Maurice." Louis called out. "It's me. Are you here? Answer me Maurice."

Maurice let out a deep sigh as the voice grew nearer and Maurice recognized that it was his friend. "Louis. That be you Louis?"

"Yeah, Maurice. Where are you? This place is falling apart and I can't see a thing."

"Here, man. Up here. Be careful of them there steps." Maurice leaned over the railing and watched the dark form of Louis take the steps two at a time. "How you be knowin' where I be?"

"I got a good memory. Did you forget how you told me about that door?" Louis followed Maurice into the room where he had been hiding. "Man. This place stinks. How do you stand it?"

"I ain't got no place else to go."

Louis stared at the horrible filth piled up in the room. "You eat here, too?" Louis looked around in disbelief and disgust.

"Sure. I sneak on out and get to my mama's and get some food. Then I be high tailin' it right back here. This be my home, Louis. This be what I call my home."

"You know what smells worse than this room is you, Maurice. God, have you got a good look at yourself lately."

"I ain't into what I be lookin' like, man. I into survivin."

"How long have you been here?"

"Since the day them cops turned me loose. I head right for mama's. I know'd Hoagy not but two steps behind me. I come right here and hide. Even my mama don't know I here."

"You know there isn't anyone who really knew what happened. I mean about what you did to Flo. I just figured you probably had more to tell. This Hoagy. Is he after you?"

Maurice lay back on the pile of papers he used for a bed. He was so weary and so tired of hiding. "Ain't nothin' be right with me, Louis. I done messed up again. I expect Loreen she be plenty mad at me."

"That's an understatement. You about fixed yourself with everyone, Maurice. Just about everyone."

"Why you come here then?

Louis looked at the floor. He couldn't bring himself to sit down. "I suppose because I'm your friend. Maybe it's like Loreen says, I haven't had long enough to get burned out on you yet. So are you hiding from this Hoagy or not?"

Maurice paused again and again as he told Louis what had happened. "Sooner or later they be gettin' me, Louis. Them dudes like that Hoagy, they don't forget nothin'."

"No," Louis agreed, "I don't expect they do." He stood next to the broken window. "You can't go on hiding here forever, Maurice. Eating all that junk and sleeping on that newspaper. You're going die up here from rat bites if nothing else."

"Don't pay me no mind." Maurice shrugged. "Every now and then mama be havin' a few dollars. I be takin' them dollars and savin' so as I can get outta here. Lookee." Maurice took a roll of bills out of his pocket.

Louis took the money and counted the bills. "You got twenty-six dollars here. What are you going to do with that? That won't even buy you a bus ticket out of here." Louis handed him back the money. "Maurice, I don't believe you. I just figured you were smarter. Why don't you just go to the police and tell them what happened?"

"What them police gunna be doin'? Arrestin' Hoagy. Ha. Hoagy too smart for that one. Ain't no way them police gunna be believin' me. What they be carin' about me anyhow. What they be carin' that Hoagy gunna get me."

"Tell them what you know. Make some kind of deal that you'll tell them all about Hoagy."

"Then what?"

"They'll arrest Hoagy and you can go back to school. You can't go on like this, man. You just can't."

Maurice stood up and went to the window where Louis now stood. "You is real smart in them books, Lou-EE, but you ain't got no street smarts. Them police got snitches comin' out of the walls. They got about as many snitches as

164

they got police. They ain't be worrin' about no Hoagy. He's nothin' out there. Probably Hoagy some kind of snitch hisself. The police let him go right on selling his drugs and Hoagy be showin' up talkin' to one of them undercover cops. Runnin' his face about them big ones that sellin' all them drugs. Hey, man, Hoagy ain't but a nothin' out there. The police they got no time for dudes like Hoagy. They's after the *man*. The big *man*."

"I don't know whether you know what you're talking about or not, Maurice. Too much craziness for me."

"I know'd I ain't leavin' here."

"I'll be back, Maurice. I'll get you some clean clothes and some food, and I'll be back."

"How Loreen and Marvin be?"

"They're fine, Maurice. Just fine. Marvin's talking now. Some counselor at school helped Loreen get him in a day care center. Loreen was missing too much school because she was having to look after him."

"That Trash Face, Carminetta. She not be helpin' Loreen no way."

"Not any more than she ever did. Marvin pretty well thinks that Loreen is his mother. He doesn't see Carminetta often enough to know who she is."

"And my Auntie Flo. How she be?"

"I don't know, Maurice. I haven't been by in a while. I guess she's okay."

"I love my Auntie Flo. Surely as I be sittin' here, I do love my Auntie Flo."

The visits to the vacant building continued through most of

the summer. Maurice would listen carefully to each piece of news that Louis brought. His feelings were mixed when Louis would leave. Maurice wanted to know how his aunt and Loreen were doing, but at the same time he realized he missed them and wanted to see them again.

As the weeks passed even Maurice came to realize that he had to leave the building and that he could no longer spend each day a prisoner of fear. He was becoming bolder about leaving the building at night to roam the streets. Then his heart would start pounding when he imagined that he saw someone following him. No matter which way he turned, he was sure that ahead of him was a young man in a blue jacket waiting to stick a knife in him. Then he'd hurry back to his hideaway.

Just before school started in the fall Louis came for one last daytime visit. "I won't be back anymore during the day. I can only come at night, and not every night at that."

"You be goin' back to school, huh?"

"My last year." Louis looked at his shoe as he rubbed it back and forth in the dirt that had once again collected on the floor that he and Maurice had cleaned up just a short time ago. "I got something to ask you, Maurice."

"Whatcha be wantin' Lou-EE?" Maurice teased and tried to laugh even though he felt very sad in knowing that it would be a while before Louis returned.

"I got some money for you." Louis reached in his pocket and took out his wallet. "It's about a hundred dollars."

"Where you be gettin' that kind of money?"

"From my job. Loreen gave some, too. She knows about you now."

166

"Loreen know'd I be here?"

"Yeah. At first she didn't want to talk about it. I told her about the jam you're in. She finally agreed to help. She...I mean it's not like I forced her or anything. She said she really wanted to help you. We want you to take this money and get yourself a bus ticket and go away for awhile. You don't have to go far. Maybe even up to Archer or to Marion. Just far enough so that you'll be safe. You can go to one of those places that are set up for runaways. Here." Louis took another paper out of his wallet. "Here's the address of a place in Archer. Here are two places in Marion. Loreen got the names from the counselor." Louis put his hands up. "Don't even ask. No. Loreen didn't tell anyone why she wanted the addresses. She just said for a friend."

"I still be Loreen's friend?"

"I think the money proves it. You know, Maurice, we all get fed up with you. You know that, don't you?"

Maurice nodded.

"Despite that, Loreen and I don't want to see anything happen to you. I was reading this thing in the paper the other night about one of these gangs. There was this horrible gang killing. They did some pretty horrible things to this dude. Loreen and me just kept thinking about you. We figured it could just as easily have been you. Neither of us want that. We decided then and there that we'd do what we could to help you get out of the city. Will you go?"

"It ain't somethin' I gotta be thinkin' about all that much. My brain has done disappeared bein' up here so long. Yeah, Louis, I'll go."

"Good."

"Now you take these addresses. With this money and that little bit you got off your mama, you can get yourself the ticket, have money for food, and maybe a place to stay until you get to one of those homes for the runaways."

"I ain't no runaway."

"Then what are you?" Louis challenged him. "And tell them the truth, too. Don't be making up anymore lies. There will come a day when you can come back. It's not like you have to stay away forever. One of these days someone is going to blow Hoagy away. You know that and I know it. Maybe he'll even forget about you."

"Them kind don't never be forgettin'." Maurice took the money. He stood beside Louis. He was thinking about the time he had eaten in the restaurant with Jean. She had told him to tell his friends how he felt. "I ain't never had no friend like you Louis. You been the kindest friend I ever be havin'. Ain't nobody stick by his friend the way you done stick by me." Maurice did something that he didn't think himself capable of doing. He put his arms around Louis and hugged him. "I gunna miss you, man. I really gunna be missin' you."

Louis' arms tightened around Maurice. "We'll miss you, too. You write us. I'm going to let your Auntie Flo know where you went. Okay?"

"Okay, man." Maurice stepped back into the darkened room.

"Now you know where to get the ticket and all that stuff."

"Sure, Louis. I know'd what I gotta be doin'."

"Bye, Big Mo."

"Bye, Lou-EE." Maurice jabbed at Louis' arm. "You be takin' care of yourself and Loreen and my boy Marvin."

Maurice watched from the window as Louis ran across the street.

CHAPTER SIXTEEN

Several days passed before Maurice could bring himself to leave the filthy, empty building that he had come to think of as his home. He slipped down the stairs and through the hidden door in the basement. The door to his mother's apartment was open slightly. Maurice pushed the door open and went to the cartons by the small cot where he used to sleep. One by one he removed each piece of clothing from the boxes and held the pants and shirts up against his body. The clothes that he had worn last year were too small or too short for him.

"Whatcha doin' there, boy?" His mother called from the doorway. She stood leaning against the door jam.

"Mama I is leavin'."

"So. Ain't you always be leavin'?"

"I leavin' for good. I come to say goodbye."

She waved at him and walked into her bedroom, slamming the door behind her.

Maurice emptied out her purse on the kitchen table and took the five dollars she had in her wallet. He felt less sadness leaving the apartment and his mother than he had felt leaving the vacant building. He slowly made his way to the bus station, carefully stopping along the way to make sure no one was following him and to make sure that no one on the street recognized him.

The bus station was crowded. Maurice glanced up at the clock, remembering how he had learned to tell time when he was at Morton Hills. The line in front of the ticket window moved quickly. Maurice was trying to think whether he wanted to go to Archer or to Marion. As he put his money on the counter he selected Archer simply because the first letter of the city started with an "A."

"When that bus be leavin'?"

"Nine-twenty. You got plenty of time."

Maurice took the ticket and shoved it into his shirt pocket. He sat down in a chair and watched the overhead television. There was a child on the program who reminded Maurice of Marvin. Maurice stood up and walked over to buy himself a soda. He wondered if he would ever see Marvin again. As quickly as the thought came into his head, he turned and walked out of the bus station. The man said there was plenty of time. Maurice was determined to use some of the time to say goodbye to Loreen and Marvin.

The walk to their apartment was taken without any care. Maurice never stopped to look where he was going or who might be on the streets. His one thought was to tell Loreen he was sorry and to hold Marvin before he left for Archer. As Maurice turned the corner he heard the screaming of fire engines coming toward him. He glanced up and saw the flames. He screamed, "Marvin." Then he ran for Loreen's building.

Smoke was pouring through the hallways. Maurice pulled off his jacket and wrapped it around his head. He groped along the hall to the second floor where he could see flames leaping and jumping along the boards that were overhead. The smoke burned his eyes and he gasped for breath.

By the time he reached the top of the stairs, he could no longer see anything. He knelt down on the floor and crawled

171

along. His knees burned with the heat coming from below him. One by one he counted off the doors that he knew were there in the hall that led to Loreen's flat. Twice he felt someone's body brush past him and he heard the unknown figures screaming. He reached the end of the hall and kicked in the door to Loreen's flat. His throat was too choked up with smoke to call out.

There was no sound in the apartment except the roaring sound made by the smoke and the crackling of the flames. Maurice staggered to his feet and made his way in what he thought was the direction of the playpen. He reached down and felt Marvin's body. "Oh, no. My little Tough Stuff. Maurice he be gettin' you out." He grabbed the baby in his arms and stumbled toward the door. As he threw open the door a wall of smoke poured in. Maurice collapsed on the floor.

Holding Marvin in his arms, Maurice tried to pull himself forward toward the window. The window was nailed closed and he had no strength or time to pull it open. He set Marvin down and picked up a lamp and smashed it against the glass.

Maurice sucked in the air that rushed into the room. He glanced down, nearly falling as he looked at the crowd and the fire engines below. "Here." He screamed. "Gotta get me help." He reached down and held up Marvin. "Marvin. Help my baby Marvin."

"Can you see the canvas?" A voice shouted. "Throw the baby. We've got him. Can you hear me?"

Maurice leaned out the window and dropped Marvin. Then he fell against the wall and tumbled to the floor.

When the firefighters reached the apartment most of the second floor had collapsed onto the floor below, Maurice was found in the first floor hallway. Maurice died along with three others. As his body was carried out, those in the crowd called out, trying to find out who was in the plastic bag. Some who stood outside the building knew who the tragic fire had taken, and they weeped for their friend.

There were so few who came to the funeral. Several teachers from Maurice's school. The superintendent from Morton Hills. Mr. Krueger. Jean. Flo. Loreen and Louis. The preacher spoke about the hero they were burying that day. About the young man who gave his life for the child. Loreen looked at Louis. It was as if both of them remembered the novel they had read in class. Louis mentioned it as they both walked toward Jean's car. "Did you think about that book?"

"Yeah." Loreen could not stop crying.

"Maurice was like that guy. It was like he knew it was a..." Louis tried to think of the line. "Far, far better thing I do now than I have ever done before. It was something like that."

"I suppose so." Loreen leaned against him to keep from falling.

Jean and Flo hung onto each other. Flo kept murmuring, "Oh, my boy. My boy is gone."

The tears falling from Jean's eyes didn't stop from the time they left the cemetery until she stood in front of Flo's house. "Do you want me to stay with you, Flo?"

"No need, child." Flo opened the door. "My children are

coming by. My daughter said she'd be here for a few days. Some place in me I know there's the strength to go on. It's got to be there. Oh, Lord, Jean, it's just got to be there."

"It'll be there for all of us." Jean kissed her and ran for the car.

Loreen and Louis sat huddled together in the backseat. Jean turned on the engine and drove off. Without realizing where she was going, she drove past the building where Maurice had died. Jean stopped to look at the charred remains of the empty building.

"Don't stop here." Loreen pleaded. "I don't ever want to see this place." She buried her face on Louis' shoulder. "I hate that Carminetta. I'll be hating her until the day I die for leaving my baby alone. Maurice would be alive now if that Carminetta had...I hate her." Loreen screamed over and over.

Jean opened the door and stepped out of the car. She walked close to the yellow plastic streamer that was strung out around the building to keep people away. For several minutes she stood there crying. Then she bent down and picked up a rock and threw it at the building. "It's places like you that take our children." She stooped again and grabbed a handful of the rubble piled on the sidewalk. Jean screamed as she kept throwing the rocks and ashes at the building. Then she knelt down and sobbed.

Louis came and knelt beside her. "Come on, Mrs. Bestie. This isn't doing you any good. Maurice was our hero. He's always going to be our hero. He saved Marvin. That's something that's pretty good."

"I know." Jean gasped. "I just hate all of this. I hate it.

I hate what these streets do to our children."

Louis looked through the car window at Loreen. "I guess there's more than enough hate to go around today, Mrs. Bestie."

It was nearly three weeks before Jean could return to the classroom. She simply couldn't bare to face more young faces. The fall semester had already started before she returned. Her friend Marilyn waved to her. Jean waved back, but could not manage a smile.

They both stood at their doors as the boys filed in. Mr. Krueger walked along behind the boys. One lagged several steps in back of the others. Mr. Krueger stood behind him and pointed to the tall boy in front of him. "We got a new one while you were gone." He made a face and whispered to Jean after the boys had entered the room. "He's a corker this one is. If he turns out to be more than you can handle, let me know."

Jean looked at the boy leaning against the wall. He refused to sit down at a desk. "Would you like to sit down over there?" Jean motioned toward an empty desk. "That desk belonged to..." Her voice choked up. "A hero. You might say the desk belonged to a hero."

"I don't be carin' nothing about no heroes." The boy slid down the wall and sat on the floor.

Jean nodded to Mr. Krueger. "It will be all right."

"Are you sure?"

"Yes. I'm sure." Jean walked to her desk and opened the drawer. From her purse she took out the newspaper clipping about the young man who had given his life to save a baby in a burning building. She wiped at her nose. Then she put the clipping on top of the poem that Maurice had written.

"I'll give you a little time." She looked at the boy sitting on the floor. "I'm sure that one of these days you might be just the one to tell me what it's like on the other side of the sun." Jean smiled at him.